Good Intentions 2:

Blind

Ambition

*Angi, thank you so much for supporting my dream. I truly hope you enjoy the ride *[illegible]*.*

-Lakinia Ramsey-

Publisher's Note: This is a work of fiction, names, characters, places and incidents are either the product of the author's imagination, or are used fictitiously, and any resemblance to actual persons, living or dead, business establishment, events, or locales is entirely coincidental.

ebook Edition: Abstract Village, 2017

Print Edition: Abstract Village, 2017

Cover Image: "Image Copyright Jumpin Sack 2016" Used under license from Shutterstock.com".

Cover Art and Design: Theopolis Ramsey, Lakinia Ramsey, and Peter Young (PY)

Dedication

GOD, thank you for it all.

A special dedication to my "first love who defined love", James O. Watts. I miss you beyond words. RIP (Rest in Power) daddy...I'll love you forever

The winds of change are blowing...new seasons are arriving...the cycles of life keep turning...With each passing year the vision of "Home" becomes less and less clear...Old soldiers are passing on...familiar faces are moving on...Sometimes I wish the world would just STOP...just a moment...to remember the laughter, to memorize faces, to capture voices...In my youth I didn't know better...I didn't know that 50 years could seem like 10...that tomorrows didn't always exist, that families fade...I didn't know better...I would have danced until the sweat poured, I would have laughed until my stomach ached, I would have talked until words ceased...I would have kissed faces, held hands, loved hearts, held on to time...but I didn't know better...now...the winds of change are blowing...a new season has arrived, and the cycle of life is slowing down...and I am not ready for it all to end.

(Lakinia Ramsey aka "First-born")

LAKINIA RAMSEY

Dedication to the Author

Wow, how do I even begin to express how I feel about this amazing, wonderful, talented author whom I've had the privilege of sharing 30 (+) adventurous years with.

We've laughed together, been a shoulder to cry on for each other...and even shared an apartment together (well I kind of just moved myself in lol). But hey you welcomed me right in!!!

Through everything we've been through you have been my best friend and the sister I've always dreamed of having.

As the saying goes, give a person their flowers while they yet live...so I would like to tell you "THANK YOU" for showing Jakavia and I so much unconditional love and helping to shape me into the woman I am today.

We've come a long way sis, but this is just the beginning. I wish you nothing but the best in whatever you set out to do and no matter where life takes you just know that I will always be your biggest fan.

As J and Cam would say "I love you to the moon and back again".

Love you always.

Your Sis,

Shaquita Wilkerson aka "Dounk"
P.S. Thank you for always being my "life-line"

LAKINIA RAMSEY

Acknowledgments

Theopolis Ramsey...I love you husband. You are **EVERYTHING**. Who would this woman be without you? You are my champion, my comforter, my motivator...my biggest fan. I'll love you forever...love is love, love.

Doshia Watts...I love you mommy. Thank you for teaching me to dream bigger than my circumstances. We've accomplished a lot together but greater is surely coming. Through the challenge of losing the love of your life, you have taught me the true and raw meaning of love. I can only marvel at your strength and courage and pray that I be just like you when, and if, I ever grow up.

To my siblings **Yasmin and Zach Watts**, I love you, I'm always here, and I'll always fight for 'us'.

Born my cousin, but raised as my sister...**Shaquita (Mitchell) Wilkerson**...we will never part. Thank you for being my first best friend. No distance could ever break our bond. Love you girl.

There would be no book without my Pit Crew. This year I was honored to have **Khara Norris, Virgilia Edge, Dani Hall and Ladona Taylor** as a part of my team. Thank-you ladies for your feedback, your edits, and your thoughts. Please know that your voices made a huge impact.

To my **Village** past and present (I won't name you all again [see book 1] but you know who you are)...God has truly blessed me with an amazing Team. I am so grateful for all of the love, support, and motivation that you all never cease to rain on me. I love you and I whole-heartedly thank you for loving me. **Curtis Rodgers, I hope you caught that cameo!

Table of Contents

Chapter 1: New Beginnings

Chapter 2: Honey

Chapter 3: Window Seat

Chapter 4: Back Again

Chapter 5: Second Chances

Chapter 6: Life Interrupted

Chapter 7: Descent

Chapter 8: Reminisce

Chapter 9: At First Sight

Chapter 10: Late Nights

Chapter 11: A Familiar Place

Chapter 12: Inner Circle

Chapter 13: Proof

Chapter 14: Changes

Chapter 15: Complexity

Chapter 16: Forbidden

Chapter 17: Sanctuary

Chapter 18: The Space Between

Chapter 19: Reality

Chapter 20: Silence

Chapter 21: Afterglow

Chapter 22: Broken Promises

Chapter 23: Pieces

Chapter 24: Naked Mornings

Chapter 25: Broken

Chapter 26: Sweetest Thing

Chapter 27: Once My Brother

Chapter 28: Sunday Morning

Chapter 29: The Endgame

"Good Intentions are the most beautiful of secrets."

-Iman Ali

I hate her.

Even though I don't really know her. I hate her. I hate this woman who has carelessly woven herself into every fabric of my life. I hate her for loving him. And sometimes, in rare moments of pure honesty, I hate him for doing what I thought could never happen...falling in love with someone else. Falling in love with her.
Toni.

Who was she to take what was rightfully mine? Because...she had taken him. I could never admit that to her, him, or anyone else...but I know it every time he touches me...every time he kisses me...every moment I catch him staring into space...so preoccupied in his thoughts that he doesn't realize that I am watching. I know. Women...no matter how adept we are at fooling others...inevitably, our instincts will not allow us to escape the ultimate truth. I smile at him...and in the cloak of darkness, I whisper sweet words of endearments.

I pretend that we have moved beyond that crater of poisonous emotions, words, and actions. But I know there is a part of him that never left Atlanta...that never completely came home, back to me.
She took it.

And I hate her for that.

--Reflections Sarai Jackson

A Year In The Life...

Chapter 1: New Beginnings

"Good morning Mr. J."

The greeting rings out from my favorite barista, Shay, who knows her regulars by name. Funny, I never used to be much of a coffee shop-type guy, but I guess in time...all things eventually change.

"Morning Shay."

Her greeting is returned with my customary nod and smile. Though some may see my gesture as overt flirtation, it never fails to earn me a free scone with my daily brew.

"The usual?" she asks, but doesn't wait for me to respond before she begins putting together my order. It's apparent that she asks more out of habit than anything else.

"Of course...a little bit of cream...a whole lotta sugar."

She always smiles when I say this. I'm not sure if her reaction is entirely due to my harmless advance or because I'm typically her nicest customer at eight o'clock in the morning.

In fact, on many mornings as this, I watch the distracted mass of rude and rushed bodies as they head off to the never ending rat race...wired and stressed before the day really even begins. Each morning, bearing witness to the endless cycle, confirms my decision to drop out early in the game. It may have appeared selfish at the time when in hindsight, it was the best decision I could have made to protect my sanity.

Shay brings me coffee along with a fresh blueberry scone. I walk over to what has become "my" table...my morning ritual once again complete.

Such is my life.

Three hundred and sixty degrees of complex evolution...only to be right back where I started; once again firmly established in the dutiful roles of father, husband and son. It is the path that I have chosen...one that I have thrown myself into. It does not mean that I am without doubts. It just means that I am resigned to my fate.

It's not that I'm unhappy. Life, at this moment, can certainly be defined as good. In truth, it has taken a lot of work getting it to this point. Still...it's good. My daughter loves having daddy home and that has always been my motivation for making things work between me and Sarai. I'm back in my father's good graces and Sarai, well I'm resigned that things between us will always be...complicated. There are good days in the Jackson household, as well as bad ones. At least there seems to be a fair balance...for now anyway. We have finally accepted the truth that we are different people...that the young lovers who married ten years ago no longer wholly exist. While there are pieces of "us" that remain, we have indeed evolved. So this year-long journey has basically consisted of us learning who we are all over again and having blind faith that love, in its truest form, will once again find itself in our midst.

Still...I think about her.

Toni.

I can't help it. Naively, I believed that being back in D.C- encased in the familiarity of home- would diminish my feelings for her and somehow, give me a new perspective.

That hasn't proven to be the case.

Try as I might, I can't forget her. How could I? In retrospect, I realize that what we shared can never be duplicated, not even with the woman I call my wife. I often wonder how is it that one woman, in such a short period of time, seems to have known and understood me better than the woman who has known me forever. Sarai has been on this journey of life with me since my college days, watching me grow from a young man to the man I am now. Toni...she gets me...all of the essential pieces of me. And I love her for that. I can't seem to stop loving her, which is the very problem that consistently plagues me.

I've spoken to her only once...even though I vowed not to. A day came when I just missed her too much not to reach out. Maybe the feelings were triggered by a song on the radio...or a random encounter on the street...I don't know...I just know that I had to hear her voice. Truthfully, I never expected her to answer the phone. But she did. At the sound of her voice, I was transported back to that time and place where love existed on a different plane...to a world of chocolate skin, poetic words, and late night whispers.

Our conversation was brief. I said a thousand "I'm sorry's" while she shed a thousand tears. What else was there to say...or do? My choice had been made...and she had moved on. It was painfully obvious that she needed nothing from me. Just as well...I had nothing to offer. My heart was heavy with the weight of unspoken words as we said our final goodbye. There's a nagging pain that lingers, yet somehow I have managed the feat of settling into the routine of my now ordinary life.

*****

Shay completes the order of her last customer and comes to join me, now cradling her own steaming cup. Her co-workers whisper in obvious, conspiratorial tones behind her retreating back.

I can't resist the opportunity to tease her. "Little girl, I'm pretty sure you have everyone in here thinking that we're having some kind of lurid affair."

She giggles in response. "I know Mr. J...I love it. These thirsty heifers would do anything to trade places with me right now. I swear if you weren't married I would really give them a show."

"Well thank you for your consideration." I laugh, taking a sip of coffee. I've been coming to this spot for months and Shay has been a constant fixture. I've come to look forward to our early morning encounters. She's pretty, young, and highly entertaining. Thankfully, she's also well aware that my interest in her is strictly limited to our brief conversations.

"Anyway...forget them" she continues. "Hopefully I'll be moving soon and I won't have to put up with any more of this foolishness."

Her off-hand statement catches me by surprise. This is the first time she has ever mentioned moving. Through our general snippets of conversations I've managed to pick up some tidbits about her personal life. I've gathered that she is close with her mom and that she has a little sister she adores. She's never mentioned her dad, and I've never asked, assuming that either through choice, death, or separation, he hasn't been directly involved in her life.

"You're leaving D.C...your family?" I question, unsure of her context of "moving."

"Yep." She confirms with unabated enthusiasm. "My boyfriend, Brian, is moving down south and I'm going with him." She pauses, uncharacteristically somber. "I need a fresh start Mr. J. If I don't get out of here soon, I'm gonna die. I'm just...stuck."

If anyone knows how she feels it's certainly this man. A life with a starved soul is no life at all...at any age.

She continues. "My mom thinks I'm crazy. She thinks I'm foolish for leaving home...everyone and everything I know...to follow a man. I can't get her to understand that I'm not just leaving for Brian. I need to do this for *me*. I have to find out if there's more to life than what I'm doing now. I don't know Mr. J...it may or may not work out...but... I'm thinking that I have to at least try. You think I'm crazy?"

Before answering, I carefully examine my response. Shay is young...impressionable. I don't want my advice to be the determining factor in this crucial decision. Yet, I realize that I can't let the moment pass to share my version of "truth."

"Shay...I don't think you're crazy at all. You have no kids, minimal responsibilities. Right now, you have a rare opportunity to live your best life. Do that. If you don't at least try you will always regret it...and life...it's just too short for regrets. Besides...you're right...if it doesn't work out, I'm sure your mom's door will still be open...just my opinion."

She seems to contemplate my solicited words of wisdom. "Thanks Mr. J. That's exactly what I needed to hear."

As she stands to leave, she gives me one last teasing smile, "I know you're gonna miss me Mr. J."

I can't t help but smile in response.

"Yeah Shay...I will miss you, my little ray of sunshine."

She laughs and marches off, satisfied with my answer. "Change is coming Mr. J. I got a feeling."

*****

Usually I linger for hours. Not today. Today I have work to do, pieces to finish.

When I reach the door, I turn to wave goodbye at Shay, who has resumed her post behind the counter. She raises a nearby coffee mug in a mock toast, "Here's to new beginnings Mr. J."

"To new beginnings Shay."

*****

My alarm is soundly ringing...rudely interrupting my restless slumber. I hate it but I can't ignore it. Monday morning. *A new day begins.* Reluctantly I sit up, reaching for my phone in the process. *8 o'clock.* If I don't hurry I will be late. Old habits, I'm finding, are way too hard to break. I force myself to abandon the comfort of my bed and sleep-walk my way into the bathroom. For a minute, I stare at my disheveled reflection in the mirror. Disheartened, I realize there is great work to be done. My hair has grown out into a tangled, wild mess of curls. I don't know what to do with it anymore. Once, briefly, I thought about cutting it off and starting over.

A new beginning.

Rae was quick to nip that foolishness in the bud. She worried that I was having some kind of breakdown over the break-up with Keenan. Maybe I was. For so many months, I had been lost. His disappearance left me void...vacant...longing. Still does sometimes. Especially on the nights when I dream of him...of our moments together. In my dreams, the silkiness of his skin is real. The sound of his laughter is real. Then, I wake up to an empty bed, and the harsh reality bitterly reminds me that he is thousands of miles away....in another life...with another woman. Dreams, even as they fade, leave their enduring mark: tangled hair...dark circles beneath my eyes, the unmistakable stain of tears dried on my face.

Although it's been a year, there are times when it still hurts like hell. When the pain emerges so raw...so piercing, that it seems like only yesterday when he walked out of my front door for good. Today though, is a new day...one that I refuse to spend dwelling on the past. I turn on the shower, my first official step in preparing for the day ahead.

Finally pulled together, I grab my travel mug and keys before hurrying out of the door. The cool breeze of fall caresses my face. While spring in Atlanta is undoubtedly my favorite season, there's something magical to be found in the fall. Beyond the beautiful earth tone colors boldly displayed, life itself seems to slow its hectic pace.

I check my watch again and realize that I'm about to be late for a meeting with Muse's primary investor, Daniel Moore. *Damn.* He's even worse than Rae when it comes to being punctual. I pray it won't take too long since I want to make it to Muse in decent time. Quiet moments in my sanctuary are exactly what I need. The broken pieces of my dream have left me in a subdued state.

The meeting with Daniel is at his office about 20 miles north of the city. Although I'm prepared to settle in for a tedious commute, traffic is unusually light. Most times we meet at Muse but Daniel's been so busy lately that his visits have become few and far between. Not that we've shifted from his line of priority. In fact, the meeting today is in regards to Muse's future. After reviewing the most recent reports, Daniel thinks it's time to expand. So much so, that he's already scouted a few possible locations. After much debate, he's roped Tanya onboard with the new developments. Me...well I'm not so sure.

On paper Muse is a business...investors, partners, numbers, dollar signs. Still, beyond the stats, it's *my* baby. Years of hard work, late nights...sacrifices...have been invested in this business. My fear is not that it will continue to grow, but that in the end it will grow beyond anything that I can control. That my

11

initial hold will diminish to a point where I no longer own what is rightfully mine. So, yeah, I'll definitely keep an open mind even as that nagging sense of caution remains.

*****

Our meeting goes longer than expected. By the time we're finished, a dense fog of mental exhaustion has thoroughly set in. It was not a simple meeting as I had anticipated. Daniel bombarded me with so many charts, forecasts, and numbers that my head is left spinning. Thank God I had coffee on deck or I probably would've walked out without a second thought.

This part of the business is outside of my normal lane. Usually, I handle the marketing components while Tanya handles the management aspects. However, with so many key decisions in place, I've been left with no choice but to be very hands-on in this process. As overwhelming and stressful as it is, I'm trying to keep it all in perspective without being biased by my personal attachments.

One thing is certain. Daniel is absolutely ready to make a big move. Somehow I thought that we were still in the "let's consider this an option" phase, while obviously he is in the "let's make it happen" phase. Things are moving way too fast for my level of comfort. I don't know. I'll just have to continue my research and see how things evolve.

*****

As I walk in, the charming ring of our bell announces my arrival. Though it's not quite noon, the store is already bustling with students and other patrons. Mia, in typical fashion, is manning the station behind the register. There's an instant look of gratitude on her face once she realizes that I am the new presence. Taking that cue, I hurry to the back to change clothes, almost running into Tanya who is rushing out of the bathroom next to our small office.

"Slow your roll girl." I tease, sliding into the office to avoid further collision.

"Sorry girl." She follows my lead and wearily collapses into the nearest chair. "We have been slammed this morning. What are you doing here so early?"

I give her a brief run-down on the meeting with Daniel while I discard my jacket, change into a company tee, and pull my hair into a messy bun. She listens attentively...never once interrupting.

"I just don't know Tanya." I finish and sink into the chair at the desk. "There are just so many variables at play."

"I know Toni." She responds. "Daniel and I already had this conversation and it's certainly a lot to consider. Truthfully though, I'm thinking expansion makes sense...at least for our long-term goal of financial stability. The hard part will be getting through the first years. The renovations, hiring new staff, the promotions...it will take a financial toll. But we've been here before girl. Think about it... it'll be like the early days of Muse all over again."

If that sentiment was supposed to be a source of comfort, it wasn't. Today we can officially claim Muse as a successful venture, but those early days were rough and on more than one occasion I considered throwing in the towel. With blind faith, we held it together, persevered and thank God we made it over. I'm certainly at a different point in my life right now though. I honestly don't know how many late nights and stressful days I have left in me.

I rub my temples...hoping to ease the symptoms of an emerging headache. It is way too early in the day for all of this.

Tanya stands up and comes around to give me a comforting hug before pulling me towards the office door. "No worries girl. None of that is happening today. Besides if we don't get out of here soon, Mia is going to kill us both and I'm not trying to get on her bad side. I'm ghosting y'all in about 30 minutes."

Reluctantly, I follow her back out to the front of the store.

Today's troubles will be put on the backburner until tomorrow.

*****

She is the first person I see when I walk into Muse.

Beautiful...always.

Her thick mane is pulled into a barely-constrained bun, exposing her pretty face. Her body is sculpted perfection in dark jeans. Even now, as I watch her, I want nothing more than to go to her and wrap her up in my arms. Touch her soft hair....inhale her sweet scent. Now, though, is not the time.

For years I've wanted her...secretly desired her....wanted so badly to be more than just her friend...her constant. Now, she is absolutely mine. The deadbeats are long gone. Keenan...is gone.

Mine.

I'm not sure why it took me so long to fight for her. Perhaps I foolishly believed she would always be there. Or maybe I just wasn't ready. What I do know is that I almost lost her...to Keenan... my cousin, my best friend...my brother. If I had lost her, there would have been no chance of getting her back. In the end, Keenan made his choice and I made mine. I chose to fight...and I won.

It wasn't an easy feat. In fact, I had almost given up on the dream of having her in my life, at least as more than a friend. Months after Keenan was gone, his spirit remained. It pissed me off that even in his absence he was a worthy foe.

For months she was lost, existing as only a mere shell of her former self. She lost weight, relied on Mia to be at Muse more often... didn't hang out as much.

Ironically... it would be the darkness he created that would bring us closer together.

Although she shut down from the world...she still welcomed me. On the nights she felt the most vulnerable and lonely, I became her anchor. Throughout the course of our lives, I've always been her best friend. When Keenan left, things between us became...different. During that dark period, I became her life-line, her personal refuge. I loved her with arms wide-open and for the first time, she accepted without inhibitions. It took a while for her to reciprocate though. Still... I waited. I waited until tears finally turned into words, words finally transformed into conversations and conversations bore witness to the first projections of laughter.

Eventually, the nightmares subsided. She stopped calling out his name while she slept. At times, I would catch her watching me with an intensity she never had before and I knew I was getting closer. Then, it happened. After one long night of wine, pizza and movies, she reached out to me, touched my face, kissed my lips, and simply whispered, "I love you."

It was everything that I had been waiting for.

*****

She sees me and silently mouths "hey." I nod in response. She's in the process of assisting a customer so I choose not to bother her. Instead, I help myself to a cup of coffee from the carafe up front, before strolling past the sea of wandering customers to a booth occupied by Mia.

"What's up Mia boo?" I tease sliding in across from her. Scattered among the table are countless books, notebooks, and other supplies...a clear indication that she's in the midst of exams. Disengaging from her book, she rubs her red-tinged, weary eyes.

"Kyle...what's up brother? I feel like I haven't seen you in forever."

"Yeah I know...it's been crazy at the office. No complaints though. What's up with you?" I ask, still taking in the chaotic scene.

She rolls her eyes. "You already know...mid-term exams. I swear I can't wait to get this year over and done with. I'm so freakin' tired and stressed man. Why...why did I think it would be a good idea to get right back in school to get my Master's? You know what? I should've been smarter. I should've left this madness behind and gotten a real job and started my real life."

I am finding her melt-down quite amusing, though, I can easily relate to her sense of desperation. It doesn't seem that long ago when I was deeply entrenched in law school. Me, Rae, and Toni had barely survived our senior year of college, but we made it...together. Law school was different. I was completely on my own. There was no one there to motivate me, push me or keep me focused. It wasn't easy but I made it through. My sheer determination and ambition to succeed carried me.

"Hang in there little sis." I try my best to reassure her. "Just try to stay focused on the end game...walking across that stage with another degree under your belt. As my mom used to tell me, education is something that once you have it, no one will ever be able to take away from you. For the record, I'm proud of you."

My words aren't spoken lightly. Mia has come a long way from her days of being the shy girl hiding out in corner booths and reciting poetry at Muse. She's really come into her own.

"Thanks Kyle. You have no idea of how much it means to have you guys constantly supporting me. Without that support, I think I would've given up a long time ago. "

"No you wouldn't have. You're way too smart and much too ambitious to settle for less. Just like your big bro." We both laugh. "Seriously, Mia, you know I'm always here for you...call me if there's ever anything you need. Aiight?"

The smile on her face lets me know that I have excelled in my brotherly duties.

"I know. That's why I love ya man."

"Love ya back." I answer, reaching across to give her hand a friendly squeeze. "Now...when do you come off break? As much as I love you, I did come here to see my woman."

In one abrupt motion, she snatches her hand back. "For real? See that's just how fast love can turn into hate." She laughs, slides out of the booth, and stomps off to find Toni. I call out after her "Nice chatting with you."

Within minutes Toni is at the table, a noticeable frown adorning her pretty face.

"Kyle, I know you didn't make Mia stop studying?" she scolds, "That girl has exams."

I muster the most innocent face I can. "I miss you babe. I just need a few minutes of your precious time. Don't deny me...please."

She shakes her head and sashays off to her office. "What am I going to do with you man?"

As soon as the door closes, I kiss her. Her taste...I don't think that I will ever get used to her taste. Her sweetness, her soft lips...it all drives me insane. We break away, both...breathless. She leans into me and wraps her arms casually around my neck.

"What did I do to deserve that sir?" she whispers.

My fingers absently caress her face. "Just being you is enough."

Her body stiffens before she eventually pulls away. It bothers me that she still does that sometimes...as if she feels smothered by the totality of my love.

"I'm just a girl." She smiles awkwardly dropping in the chair behind the desk. I move to sit on the adjacent sofa.

Noting how uncomfortable she is, I completely change the subject. I take note of the vast papers scattered across the desk. It doesn't take me long to realize they are financial reports. My interest is piqued. We don't talk much about the business of Muse, yet, from everything I do know, it's doing well.

"Everything ok?" I cautiously inquire.

"Yeah...it is." She answers with a deep breath. "Business at Muse is actually really good. Tanya did a great job managing the operation while I was...gone. So good in fact that Daniel and his partners at EBS want to expand. We've just been reviewing reports to see if it's even fiscally possible."

"That's fantastic news Toni. You don't sound excited about it though."

There is a hint of caution in her voice. "Muse is my baby Kyle. I love where we are right now in the business. We're profitable. We're making waves in the community. It's...perfect.

I'm scared that the more levels we achieve, the less control I will have. And I'm just not in a mental space to relinquish that yet."

I get it. Beyond the business, Muse is Toni's life. Coffee, art, poetry, politics...all of her passions, combined into this one dream job. She will always want to have control of that. Still, in this day and age, it's hard for small businesses to compete against the larger chains. Muse has done good business. The question still remains: for how long?

"Look, love. I don't want you to feel pressured into making moves that you are uncomfortable with, but we both know that Daniel is a savvy businessman. If you didn't trust him, you wouldn't be in business with him."

"That's all true Kyle. I do trust Daniel. I just can't shake these reservations."

There's a moment of contemplative silence when, without warning, she suddenly walks over and straddles my lap. "That's enough about business. How about we steal a few minutes before I go relieve Mia?"

I wrap my arms around her slender waist...lean in to kiss her waiting mouth.

"Let her wait."

Chapter 2: Honey

At long last, I have my groove back...and I plan on keeping it. I stand, inhale, and gaze around the crowded room. The energy is electric and intense. Things at The Paul Agency are looking up. Tonight, this...this is all because of me. The party atmosphere, the festive balloons, the flowing champagne, the gorgeous people...it's all because I have put in the work and made it possible.

Two months ago I landed a huge client, Tyler Cole, star running back of the Washington Redskins. It proved to be a move that further solidified The Paul Agency as the most prominent public relations/marketing firm in D.C. Now, here we are celebrating the launch of his new commercial ad campaign. This...is a very big deal. This one client can broaden our scope of work with professional players. While we have quite a few baseball clients, largely due to Marcus' influence, Tyler is our first legitimate NFL star. So many new doors are bound to be opened...all because of me.

Marcus Paul, my boss, the man who has pushed, prodded, and mentored me to this stage of success, catches my eye from across the room. Even among a crowd of people he is a commanding presence. Tall, dark, extremely handsome...impressively confident. He is a man who wears his success well. A lifetime ago he told me to stick with him and he would take me straight to the top. He made good on his promise.

I, on the other hand, almost faltered.

Almost.

He raises his glass and nods his head. I raise mine back in return. The expensive, effervescent liquid is cool, tantalizing, as it slides down the length of my throat. I recognize the gesture for what it truly represents...Marcus' silent acknowledgement of a job well done. At last, after a long, exhausting, tumultuous year, I can exhale. My life is being fashioned into where I envisioned it years ago when I was just a young, naïve girl on a college campus.

Out of the corner of my eye I catch the shadow of someone approaching.

Keenan.

My husband...the father of my beautiful daughter. The man who once swept a young, naïve girl off of her feet with late night whispers dripped in honey and promises of the moon and stars.

I can only laugh to myself when I think of "her". *Silly girl,* I chastise myself. Your mother tried to tell you better, but you wouldn't listen. Your mother tried to warn you that the ways of men would disappoint you every time, but you wouldn't listen. You put your faith in him. You loved him.

And he failed you.

"Hey babe." He easily greets me, leaning in to kiss me on my cheek. "Sorry I'm late. Traffic was hell trying to get downtown."

I smile at him.

Beautiful him.

In a year's time, he has evolved from the man he once was. He is more assured, more confident. I hate this transformation and love it all at the same time. While I'm thrilled that he no longer resembles the man who was once lost in his own head, this man ...this man found himself through the embrace and love of another woman. *She* made this man, not me...and I will never forgive him for that...or her.

Funny, he was a man I once loved with everything in me.

Until he failed me.

Now, that love is cautious, conditional. I embrace it, but I don't live by it...don't breathe it. He just doesn't know it. No, he doesn't know that this girl has learned from past mistakes and she will not make them again.

"No worries love." I easily respond. "You're just in time. The party's just getting started."

*****

After hours of dancing, mingling, and drinking, we stumble wearily into the house. As always Keenan's parents were fine with keeping Zy'riah for the night, so we are blessed with time alone in an empty house.

I turn on the lights and kick off my shoes all at once. I can't wait to unwind, even though my body is wired from the night's events. Keenan makes his way to the kitchen. "You want anything to drink?" I hear him ask as I cross the threshold into our bedroom, already dismissing my clothes.

"Please." I answer trying to find something easy to put on. I grab a thin, hooded tee, not even bothering to find pants to conceal my black lace panties. Between the high from the night and the alcohol, I am feeling confident and sexy. All I want in this moment is to have an intimate night with my husband.

When I walk back out, I'm surprised to find Keenan with his shirt already discarded. Music is playing softly in the background, as the subtle fragrance of ginger peach candles permeate the air. He walks towards me with purpose...a glass of wine extended for the taking. My breath catches in my throat as I grab it with trembling hands. He is and has always been insanely sexy. Even after ten years of marriage, my body still responds with ease to the mere sight of him. His silky, smooth, chocolate skin glows in the muted light...his dreads blanket his broad shoulders and back in a thick cascade of coils.

My heart is guarded...yet... I still love him. I've loved him since he was a boy really...when we were passionate with innocent love. It was exciting then...learning how to love each other. Then, real life interrupted stolen moments and somehow we lost our way.

Still, I love him.

He studies my face as I take a sip of the wine he has offered. As he leans in close, the intoxicating scent of his cologne washes over me. I close my eyes and breathe him in.

"I love you." His careless words ring in my ear.

Honey-dripped whispers.

He finds no answer. I don't need his words. Empty promises won't diminish the growing ache between my legs. Instead, I pull his beautiful face toward my own.

I need...more.

I kiss him...and that very first taste leaves me hungry for more. He groans as I feast on his delectable, full lips. Without disengaging, he removes the glass from my hand, deftly placing it on the nearby bar. My hands, now free from distraction, briefly caress his sculpted shoulders before traveling down to his narrow, belted waist.

He breaks away and hastily snatches my tee over my head. I gasp as my erect nipples are exposed to the cool air.

He reaches for me.

I reach back.

Together we follow the dimly lit path to our bedroom.

I climb onto our massive bed and lie back...waiting.

My husband...my first love who defined love.

I watch him as he removes the remainder of his clothing...admire him as he steps forward, gloriously naked. He comes to me. I find myself whimpering in anticipation. He tugs at my saturated panties, pulling them down and off to the floor. His hands hold my leg hostage as he leaves a trail of slick kisses from my ankle to my inner thigh. I cry out and squirm beneath his subtle assault. I grab a fistful of dreads and pull him in closer to my liquid heat. He holds back...refuses me this pleasure.

"Sarai," he whispers my name. "Look at me." I open my eyes. They are met by his smoldering gaze.

"I love you." *Honey-dripped whispers.* Enticing me with their empty promises.

He needs this right now, but it's not what I want. Forcefully, I pull him up to face me. His body now covers the entire length of mine...his engorged dick rests between my quivering legs.

"Fuck me."

The stain of hurt marks his face. There are moments when I can love him with the complete abandonment of our past.

Not tonight.

"Fuck me Keenan." The hurt is gone now, replaced by a raw and vengeful lust.

Before I can catch my breath, he penetrates me with commanding force. I cry out. My head is spinning...the room...the room is spinning. I claw at his shoulders as he pounds into me over and over and over again. In this state, he takes no mercy on his wife.

He grabs my ass...I bite his shoulder. The erotic mix of pain and pleasure has me spiraling out of control.

"Keenan, Keenan, Keenan!" I scream his name, daring him to claim me. My husband responds as only he can. He knows every spot, every zone. There is not one that he leaves untouched.

Before long, I am overcome by sensations. "Don't move, don't move" I beg as I start my final descent. He finds me on the journey and we ride the wave together. Our release is long...hard...gratifying.

I don't know how long it is before we move or speak. My body is aching and sore from our encounter. This is exactly what I needed.

It's hard to gauge where he is, what he's feeling. His beautiful face is masked by his curtain of dreads. I stroke his back...wait for a response. Other than the rise and fall of his soft breaths, there is nothing. He needs more...expects more.

"Keenan."

"Yes," he answers, still not facing me.

"I love you too."

Honey-dripped whispers...empty promises.

Chapter 3: Window Seat

Even after all of these months, it still feels strange waking up in Kyle's bed. I can't explain it. Always...there's this unsettling feeling I get when my eyes first open. It's not how it was when I was with Keenan. That first night I stayed at his apartment it was strange...different. Afterwards, there was never a time when I didn't feel like I was home. Now, in this space, I don't get those same feeling of comfort and security. There's some inner spirit that won't let me be at peace. And for the life of me I can't put my finger on it. What I do know is that I have to figure it out soon because even though he has not said anything, Kyle knows. There's a part of him that's always known all of me and he knows that I'm not at peace. I catch him watching me sometimes with those piercing eyes of his. I always look away...always...because I have no answers for him. So we continue to act like the big white elephant in the room does not exist and that keeps us in a place of peace...for now at least.

It's not that I don't love him. Loving Kyle, in this wonderfully, different, way, has been good for my soul. He has proven to be loving...romantic...attentive...everything that I need. There is no doubt that he loves me completely and unconditionally. So how can I help not loving him? He deserves to have me love him. Yet...loving him is *different*.

Truthfully, I can't say how long it will take for him to erase the imprint of Keenan. His touch, his kisses...they left such an indelible mark. I want so badly to give this man all of me...but my body often betrays me. Even now, in random moments, when a familiar song sifts through the radio, or I see a hint of familiarity in another's chocolate tone, I am reminded of him. And when my mind remembers, my body yearns. I know that I will never completely love Kyle until Keenan is out of my system. I just never fathomed that it would take this long.

I shift in the window seat...watching him sleep as I mindlessly drink my first cup of the morning. There is no denying his beauty. His lips are slightly parted as he softly exhales. His long lashes and thick eyebrows are a nice complement to his caramel skin. My heart aches as I watch him. I know that I don't deserve him, but I'm thankful that he is patient enough to love me still...until I can reciprocate entirely. Today though, I can only give what I have.

I place my cup on the seat and move towards the bed. Hastily I discard his shirt...one that I had quickly grabbed before my trek into the kitchen. I pull back the covers and sidle my naked body against the comforting warmth of his. He stirs when he feels me next to him. Even without opening his eyes, he reaches for me and pulls me in close. My body instantly reacts to his masculine scent...an intoxicating mixture of heat, sweat and lingering cologne. I entwine my arms around his neck and snuggle close. My body reacts to his...his, in turn, reacts to mine. He wants me...still, in spite of all of my flaws, in spite of knowing that another man still holds a piece of my heart.

He wants me.

In this moment, I love him more than ever. Softly I caress his face, relishing in its softness. A smile plays on his lips, indicating that he is now more awake than asleep. He opens his eyes...his smile widens.

"Good morning beautiful."

I smile back, unable to resist his charm. "Good morning love."

That is the beginning and end of our verbal exchange. I kiss him forcefully, while his hands begin their familiar quest of my yearning, aching body.

*****

Satiated, *check*. Satisfied, *check*. Fulfilled, *check*.

Kyle has not been in a disappointment in that area. With our scent still lingering on my skin I again re-dress in his shirt and head to the kitchen to prepare breakfast. Today is one of our rare days off. Tanya and Daniel are both going to be at Muse so there is no reason for me to go in. Surprisingly Kyle doesn't have any pressing cases to catch up on so we are rewarded with an occasion to spend the entire day together.

On past Saturdays, I would normally be on my way, late as usual of course, to Café Intermezzo for brunch with Rae and Dawn. Life, as it often will, has served up a multitude of interruptions. Therefore, the interludes between our weekly gatherings have steadily increased. With Lexie now taking dance classes and Rae working on a special project for work, it's proven hectic finding free time. Hopefully we'll be back on track soon. I miss my girls. At least we check in with each other via phone several times a week.

That's if Dawn isn't wrapped up with Jamie.

I'll admit, that reconciliation caught me by surprise. Even now, I find it strange seeing them back together as a married couple. Having Jamie back in our midst is taking a major adjustment. It's tough accepting a guy back into the fold after having personal knowledge of his transgressions. Apparently, Dawn could forgive and move forward. Nevertheless, Rae and I are still cautious. I'm just glad to see Lexie happy. Since his return, she once again gets to bask in the role of daddy's girl.

For both of their sake I hope that he's genuine. The last thing they need is for him to fail them...again.

*****

Kyle comes sauntering into the kitchen, just as I am plating our food and replenishing my coffee. His lean body is glistening with the lingering mist from his shower.

"Thank you love. This smells so good. Your man is hungry after you made him put in all that work," he teases. I make my way around the counter to sit next to him at the bar.

"And work you did baby. Just know that your girl appreciates you."

"You better." He cautions, kissing me lightly on the forehead.

We devour our food in comfortable silence. This is one aspect of our relationship that I'm glad we haven't lost...our ability to be comfortable in each other's presence. As lovers, we have not forgotten how to be friends. In that, I find a great deal of security.

"What do you want to do today?" His voice breaks through the silence.

I haven't given it much thought. We're definitely doing "something." It's fall in Georgia, which is a beautiful time to be out. While the air can still be humid on some days, it is nothing like the repressive heat of summer. It is not the time to be cooped up in the house...even with a housemate as gorgeous as Kyle.

"I haven't thought about it. Maybe can go down to Atlantic Station...do some shopping, grab some lunch. I'll call the crew to see if they want to go bowling at The Alley. We haven't had a fun night out all together in a minute."

"Works for me. I'll call them while you go shower and dress because your ass is slow as hell."

Playfully, I slap him on the shoulder before hurrying towards the master bathroom. As I discard my clothes and struggle to pin my hair, his cell begins to ring. Just before I turn on the water, he answers.

"What's up Keenan."

Damn.

Chapter 4: Back Again

I can't wait to get home. Today has been extremely exhausting. I have a show coming up at a local gallery and putting it all together has been tiring and nerve wracking. As an artist, there's nothing more exhilarating than getting an opportunity to share your gift with the world.

There's also nothing more terrifying.

Art is so insanely personal. In each work there's a reflection of some part of you. Sharing it with the world garners all kinds of attention, good and bad. Of course the good is well, good. But the bad...the harshness, the critical judgments...can often feel like a personal attack.

This traffic is not helping to resolve my bad mood. Trying to navigate my way through these convoluted D.C. streets is seemingly an impossible task. I check the time. *Damn.* I'm supposed to pick Zy'riah up from her after-school program by six. If I'm not there, we will incur a late charge. If we incur a late charge, I'll have to endure a lecture from Sarai. I am, most definitely, not in the mood for that.

With only minutes to spare, I finally arrive. Thankfully there are parking spaces available near the front, since most parents have already come and gone. My daughter runs to me when she sees me. Her teacher, Ms. Drew, is slightly less than enthusiastic. She purposefully strides towards me, a slight frown creasing the forehead of her pretty face. I'm always amazed at how young Zy'riah's teachers are. Growing up, our teachers were matronly and strict. Now, I feel as if some of them could be my own kids. Over time, though, Ms. Drew has proven to be more than qualified and could even be as strict as some of my old educators. I've probably received as many scoldings from her as some of her students, especially since this is not the first time that I've been late. Before she starts in, I try and head off the impending lashing with one of my most disarming smiles. The creases in her forehead smooth over and she returns mine with one of her own. *Disaster averted.*

"Mr. Jackson, I don't know what I'm going to do with you. Keep this up and I'm going to demand your presence in after school detention." There's an obvious hint of flirtation in her tone.

"I know Ms. Drew. I owe you tremendously," I answer apologetically.

We chat briefly about upcoming projects, before she gives me Zy'riah's report for the week and me and baby girl are on our way.

My earlier train of thought takes a backseat, as Zy'riah's ceaseless chatter infuses the air. Oh to be young again with no worries other than bad cafeteria food and the latest artistic projects. The traffic has somewhat cleared allowing us to get home within thirty minutes. When we pull into the driveway, the first thing I notice is Sarai's vehicle blocking the entrance of the garage door. Surprising, since she has been putting in late hours at the office.

In typical fashion, Zy'riah hastily discards her book bag and jacket as soon as we enter the house. Before I can chastise her, she's already rushed upstairs to her room. Curiosity steels me in the opposite direction in search of my wife.

I find her in the kitchen preparing dinner. Another surprise since she's not much of a cook. Usually I'm the one preparing dinner or at least ordering in. I hope that all of this truly reflects her mood.

At times, I brace myself before entering our home, never knowing what Sarai I'm going to confront. Some days I get the loving Sarai, the person who closely resembles my college sweetheart. Then, just when I think we've reached a turning point in our relationship, I'll unexpectedly get resentful Sarai, the unforgiving, scorned wife. The inconsistency of her moods keeps me from getting truly comfortable in our precariously mended relationship.

She turns towards me as I enter the kitchen, greeting me a radiant smile.

"Hello love."

Her affectionate attempt does not go unnoticed. I breathe a sigh of relief.

"Hey," I state, before closing the space between us, engulfing her in a genuine hug. She smells good even though her perfume subtly clashes with the fragrant aromas.

"What are you doing home so early?" I question. "I figured you would be spending another long night at the office."

"Yeah I thought so too," she answers, her attention now back on her preparations. "Negotiations with a major client were going nowhere, but they finally signed the last contract we sent over. I'm just glad to have it over and done with."

"I really hope Marcus appreciates your worth Sarai. You are a tremendous asset to his agency. I would guess his best asset."

Once again she faces me. Her eyes watch me closely before she speaks. "You know, we would have made a great team Keenan. We could have risen in the ranks...opened our own firm. Imagine...Jackson and Jackson. Just so much wasted potential."

There it is...that trace of resentment that rears its ugly head now and then.

"Not my life Sarai."

"Right...not your life. Well, anyway, there is something I want to talk to you about. Marcus has made a proposition that I need to discuss with you."

Ah ok. That explains her attempt at dinner. She is trying to prepare me for whatever "news" she has in store for me. Knowing Sarai, she would be receiving another promotion, meaning she would be spending even less time at home. At times it feels as if she is married more to her career than to me. I'm not angry, in fact, far from it. She has never been without that ambition. Not for the first time, I wish that our dreams were more aligned. Our separate paths often make me wonder if we can ever exist on one accord.

I search her face for any hints. A coy smile is all that I get.

"Why are you looking at me like that?"

"You know why. Your 'news' is not always good news for me, or even 'us' for that matter."

"I know. This is different. It's such a huge opportunity for me Keenan. Look, why don't you get Zy'riah washed up so we can eat. There's plenty of time to have this discussion."

On command, I leave to gather our daughter while trying to keep my anxiety at bay.

*****

The conversation is light fare as it always is whenever Zy'riah's around. She's at that age where she soaks up information and emotions like a sponge. Afterwards, Sarai gets her prepped for bath and bed. While I wait for her to return, I get a bottle of wine and glasses. Somehow, I'm pretty sure that whatever Sarai needs to discuss with me will digest better with a glass of Chardonnay. When she returns, her work attire has been dismissed for more casual sweats and a t-shirt and her pretty face is now void of makeup. Moments like this are when she most reminds me of the girl I fell in love with back on Howard's campus.

Carelessly, she drops like dead weight onto the sofa. There is a reflection of weariness in her eyes. Before she even has to ask, I pour her a glass of wine from the chilled bottle. I pour myself one as well and take a long sip before carefully placing it on the closest end table. She stretches out her long legs across my thighs and I take that as a hint to massage her feet.

"Thank you...that feels so good. I'm so exhausted. These past few days have been entirely too long and much too stressful."

"So?" I ask. I'm ready to get this conversation over and done with. There is no need to let it linger.

She pauses, but only momentarily. "I had a meeting with Marcus today. He and the partners are pleased with my work, especially my handling of Tyler Cole's account."

Yep...just what I thought.

She continues. "He wants to expand the market and he is considering opening a new office."

A new office? What exactly does that mean?

She stares, unblinking, before continuing. "Keenan they want to open a new office in Atlanta and they want me to manage it."

Atlanta.

There's dead silence and a moment of disbelief as I futilely attempt to gather my thoughts.

"Keenan, do you understand what I'm saying to you? They want me to move to Atlanta."

Toni. Back to Atlanta...back to her.

After some time, I find my voice. "Sarai you can't be serious. We are just now getting our lives back on track. Why in the hell would we move? To Atlanta of all places? That doesn't make sense."

Her face instantly hardens into an emotionless mask. "Funny, Atlanta seemed to fit your needs perfectly fine. Now that I need to move, for me, for my career, you have a problem with it. That's not fair Keenan."

I rub my hands over my face. There it is again, that trace of resentment that always seems to be lurking just beneath the surface. No matter how good I am or what I say, it is always there. Yet, she still wants...this?

This can't be happening.

"So you mean to tell me that your ambition is over-ruling your common sense. Why would you want me to move back to the city where..." My voice trails off. I can't do this. I've spent all day trying to rid my mind of all thoughts of Toni. This conversation is taking me to a place that I don't want go.

Her voice rises in anger. "Say her name Keenan. Why are you tip-toeing around her name? This should be easy for you."

I can only stare at her, trying desperately to find the right words. "Sarai, there is nothing about that situation that was *easy*. That's why I don't understand why you want to move. There is nothing in Atlanta for us but the fragments of hurt, pain, and anger. We are in a different space now."

Tears form in her eyes...the last thing I want to deal with.

"Do you think this is easy for me? The last thing I want is to take you back to her territory. Aside from that Keenan, I have worked my ass off for years for this promotion. I refuse to allow *Toni* to dictate my household. I can't give her that much power."

Her level of anger escalates in intensity. *Damn*. This is the last conversation I imagined us having. Although we have never had the discussion, I know that her biggest worry is the possibility of me changing my mind about working on "us". It can't be easy for a wife to hear that your husband has fallen in love with another woman. Sex, that's one thing... love is something else entirely.

This makes her announcement seem especially crazy and irrational. Why would she want me to go back...*there*?

"Sarai," Speaking her name in a quiet tone, I hope to instill a sense of calmness to the situation. "Surely there is another way around this. I mean you don't have to go to Atlanta. I know Marcus. In the next year he'll be ready to expand in another city. Let's just wait to see how it all pans out."

She is silent for a few minutes before looking at me face to face. "I don't know if I'll get another chance to prove myself Keenan. While you were gone, I messed up. I couldn't focus...I...I couldn't think...I wasn't my best and Marcus picked up on that. Giving me this opportunity is his way of showing me that he still believes in me. If I turn him down, I may not get a second chance."

My conscious is overcome with feelings of shame and guilt. In those crazy months I was so engrossed in my own mental turmoil that I never thought about how the separation impacted her on a professional level. Sarai has always been the one to have it all together; it never occurred to me that her shit could have been falling apart.

Her tear-stained face breaks my heart.

"I'm sorry."

"I know Keenan." Her voice is now a quiet whisper. "Believe me when I say that this situation is the last thing I expected, much less wanted. Still, I *have* to do this. My professional career depends on me being able to pull this off. I have to believe that you...us...we're strong enough to handle this. Can *you* handle this?"

She searches my face for answers that I can't give. Am I strong enough? Now, sitting here in front of her, it seems so easy to say yes. Yet...there is a part of me that's not so sure. How would I react once I was back in her presence? When and if, that magnetic force attempted to suck me back in, could I resist?

My wife needs me to say yes. Right now she needs her husband to reassure her that he is all in. I lean towards her waiting, beautiful face...kiss her full, soft lips.

"Yes."

The smile on her face is worth the lie.

Atlanta. Toni. Kyle.

Damn, here we go again.

Chapter 5: Second Chances

"Morning sunshine...seems like I'm right on time."

With painstaking effort, I raise my head from my desk as Marcus's rich voice echoes throughout my office...much too loud for this early, early morning. I'm sure every ounce of frustration is written on my face. The past few days have not been easy. There is tension in my home.

"Must you always be so loud?" My complaint falls on deaf ears, as I mercifully reach for the double-shot latte he extends. He closes my door and wastes no time making himself at home in one of my over-sized leather chairs.

"What's wrong? With the offer I made you, you should be floating on cloud nine. Instead, you're sitting here looking stressed as hell."

The offer.

About a week after the party, Marcus called me into his office for a meeting. I had been on edge all week, knowing it was coming. In fact, everyone in the office knew it was coming...the promotion that I had been waiting for...groomed for. At long last, it was about to happen.

Closing the deal with Tyler Cole and scoring him the lucrative ad campaign was a huge deal that could not go unnoticed...or unrewarded. It was just a matter of how and when. It was difficult to contain my excitement...although I knew that the promotion would, inevitably, be a blessing and a curse. The financial reward would be significant, that I was sure of; however, I also knew that it would come with greater responsibilities, longer hours...more sacrifice. Truthfully, I wasn't sure how much more sacrifice my relationship with Keenan could withstand.

It's not that we're not in a good place. We are...good. Yet, no matter how hard we try, we just can't seem to get back to where we were before...*her*. Were there problems before her? Absolutely. I've always been ambitious and focused on becoming a success. Admittedly, Keenan suffered for that. He didn't get it. He didn't get that being a Black woman, even one at a Black-owned agency, meant that I had to work ten times harder than anyone else. I had to work earlier mornings, later nights, and even sacrifice weekends, when other associates were home with their children and significant others. I couldn't make him get it...and I wasn't willing to change. So we drifted apart. The more we drifted, the more I buried myself in work.

It proved to be a disastrous cycle.

I never planned on her.

The whole Toni situation completely blind-sided me. The separation was tough, but I understood it. We needed space before we reached that point of no return. We had gotten in a space where we spent too much time being angry and I was afraid that we would say too much that we couldn't take back, do too much that we would regret. We just needed space to breathe.

Then, out of the blue he announced that he was moving to Atlanta with Kyle. I was shocked. Yes, we needed space, but I never imagined we would end up living in different cities. I would have never thought that he would have moved away from his parents, from Zy'riah...from me. I knew then...how wide the chasm had developed between us. For the first time I came to the realization that we may not make it.

Then he fell in love with her...and our fate was sealed.

Almost.

My mother didn't raise me to lose. I fought, and I won. He came back home to me...to our family, and we have tried to rebuild.

Still, I'm not a foolish woman. Once...not anymore. I know him, even though he's a changed man...I still know him...and I know he thinks about her. He doesn't realize that I know, but I'm aware of her ghostly presence. Her essence still lingers over us, even with her being thousands of miles away.

Now, this promotion could very well send us right back to that place. So yeah I am excited, but that excitement is rightfully laced with caution.

I never planned on Atlanta.

Marcus first hit me with the news that he had finalized details of expanding the office. I always knew that was his overall plan, but I thought it was more of a long-term goal. Then he hit me with the offer of becoming the branch manager of the new Atlanta office.

To say I was stunned is an understatement. I had no idea that he was even considering me for such a huge role. Especially after the year I'd had. The offer...was way beyond my expectations.

But...Atlanta? Oh the irony.

I thanked Marcus profusely for the opportunity, though I couldn't give him an answer; at least not until I'd spoken with Keenan.

As of today, he was still waiting.

*****

"So?"

I tune back in, just in time to catch Marcus watching me keenly. I try to come up with anything, any word to indicate that I was listening. It's pointless.

"So...what?"

An exasperated look crosses his face. "So what? So are you accepting my offer or not Sarai? I've given you days and you still haven't accepted. I thought this is what you wanted."

"No...it is Marcus" I give him what I hope is my most sympathetic face. "I'm sorry." I straighten up in my seat and take a long sip of the steaming brew.

I don't know why I haven't given him my answer. Keenan said yes. In spite of that, there is something about his hesitation that makes me nervous. I needed more time to think. Is this promotion worth risking my marriage? There was a time when the answer would have been a resounding "No". Now, things are different. He was selfish with his needs, so maybe it's time to be selfish with mine.

"Well, I need an answer a.s.a.p. I'm ready to get the ball moving and right now I can't do that if I don't know whether or not I have a manager in place."

"I know Marcus. I know."

"You know?" He asks, leaning forward in his seat. "Do you really know?"

"Yes, I do." My voice comes through barely above a whisper.

Marcus Paul can be funny and charming, but when it comes to his business, he is dead serious. His career path was once completely different than it is today. At one point in his life, he was a rising star in the major leagues; that is until he was permanently side-lined with a knee injury. He could have easily given up and become another statistic: a broke and broken former athlete, fallen from grace. Instead, determined to succeed, he turned his tragedy into a triumphant story. Two years into his forced retirement, he started The Paul Agency with his savings, and the rest...as they say, is history. When it comes to his business, Marcus has earned a reputation for being ruthless. It's hard to argue with his tactics, especially with the level of success he's garnered. With that being said, I know, in spite of our relationship, that he wouldn't hesitate to cut ties with me if I couldn't live up to his vast expectations.

Especially, with so much at stake.

He resumed his initial position in the chair. "Tell me what's going on so we can fix this."

So I tell him. *Everything.* There's a part of me that cautions to hold back. However, the past year has taking a toll on my mental status and I am ready to share that load. After I finish spewing out my complicated story of separation, love and infidelity, I can see that Marcus is struggling to come up with a response.

"Wow...Sarai I really don't know what to say. I mean I knew that you guys had gone through the separation. I had no idea someone else was involved. If I can be frank, being the strong woman you are, I'm surprised you took Keenan back."

There it is...that piteous look that I have tried in vain to avoid.

"Don't do that Marcus. Don't look at me like that."

I hate Keenan for doing this to me...making me feel shame in loving my own husband. I never thought that I would be *that* woman. My image, one that I have worked exceptionally hard to create and maintain, is one of a strong, ambitious woman who has it all together. The moment that Keenan walked out, that image was put in jeopardy. The moment he fell in love with someone else, it was almost irrevocably damaged.

"He's my husband Marcus, and I love him. I know that's not easy for everyone to understand, but I have worked too hard for my career and my family to have that stolen away. That does not make me weak...it makes me human. Besides, if anything, being backed into this corner has given me the opportunity to do what I do best...come out fighting."

I hope he sees strength underneath the chaos.

"There she is!" He suddenly exclaims. "There's the woman I've invested all of my time, energy and money in. That's the woman I need to get us to the next level. Say the word Sarai. Say yes."

I pause momentarily; once again thinking of the possible consequences of my decision.

My husband...my ambition.

In the back of my mind I hear my mother's voice. *"the ways of men will fail you."*

"Yes." I answer with conviction.

He blesses me with a brilliant smile. "Well, let's go build an empire then."

Chapter 6: Life Interrupted

Well, it's official...my ass is moving back to Atlanta. It's been three incredibly long weeks since Sarai convinced me to make the move. Against my wishes and against every instinct I have warning against it. I gave up and gave in. So we'll move and somehow I'll find a way to live in the same city as Toni. Of course I don't see how that will be possible with the added complication of her and Kyle's relationship, nonetheless, I'll manage.

Kyle. I had to call him to let him know that I was coming back. As expected, he was anything but ecstatic. It's funny how the dynamics of our relationship have changed in such a short period of time. Almost a year ago, he was begging me to move to his city....for us to be closer not only in proximity but close enough for mental support. Then...I was his cousin, his brother. Now, things are definitely different. Beyond the love and the ties that bind our relationship, is the knowledge that I am a threat to his new life...with the woman he loves. I hate it. I would be a liar if I said I didn't. I love my cousin but there is a part of me that will always remain selfish when it comes to Toni. I will always want a part of her to remain mine. I need to know that there's a piece of her heart that still carries me in it...some part that Kyle will never claim.

When I gave him the news of my return, he was understandably speechless. Always the thinker; I could actually hear the thoughts spinning wildly around in his head. He didn't ask but I know he wondered if I would come for her. And I'm sure he also wondered if she would respond. Let him live in that fear. Not that I would go to her. That will just be the price he pays for loving her...for choosing her...for hurting me. There will be a part of me that will never forgive him for that. Selfish, yet true.

In true character, Kyle is still Kyle. Without my solicitation, he offers to help us find a place to rent so that the relocation process can be as seamless as possible. Issues aside, I appreciate him for that. One thing for certain, this move will be ...interesting.

I have not told my parents about moving back to Atlanta. That conversation will be a difficult one to have. For the past months, they have gotten acclimated to having me back home. Losing me again is one thing...I can't even imagine how they are going to feel losing Zy'riah, the light of their world.

As I pull up to the house, I see my dad outside working on my mom's flower garden. I swear that man never sits still. I guess it's what keeps him young at heart. When he sees me he stops his task at hand and rises to his feet.

"Hey Pops."

"Hey Son."

We warmly embrace before making our way to the cracked and worn stoop, a spot where Kyle and I spent so many of our childhood afternoons.

"Pops do you ever sit still? I swear you're either in the streets or in this yard." He laughs easily.

"Only on Sunday son." Football Sunday would be the only thing to keep him in that recliner of his all day.

I inquire about Mom's whereabouts and he informs me that she has gone shopping. *Damn.* I'm reluctant to dive into the purpose of my visit without her present. She has an uncanny way of balancing Pop's emotions.

"What brings you out anyway? I thought you weren't coming by until the weekend?"

I take note of the curious look on his face. Not much gets past his powers of observation. I look away for a minute, trying to gather my thoughts.

"Yeah Pops, I have some news that I wanted to share with you and Mom but I guess I'll lay it on you."

"Oh yeah?" He glares at me with his piercing eyes. "What kind of news?"

How is it that no matter how old you get, with one look your parents can turn you into a fearful adolescent.

"I'm moving to Atlanta Pops." The weight of my words hangs heavy in the atmosphere. It seems like forever before he responds, while in reality it is only a few minutes.

"Atlanta? What do you mean you're moving to Atlanta?" Deep frowns crease his weathered forehead as he tries to make sense of what I'm saying. He is definitely not making this easy on me. "Boy, are you telling me that you are leaving your family again to be with that woman? I know that's not what you're saying." Although I know that he doesn't have a clear understanding of the situation...his words sting just the same. Not for me...for Toni.

That woman" Even though we are not together, I still feel the need to protect her against my dad's unwarranted judgment.

"Pops please...don't call her 'that woman'." His icy glare is beyond disapproving. "You think I care what her name is? I can care less what her name is son. All I know is 'that woman' seems hell bent on destroying your family and it seems like you're being foolish enough to let her do it." His voice spikes in pitch and it's evident that he is angry. I need to clear this situation up before it goes any more left than it has already.

"Calm down Pops, it's not even like that...just to be clear "we" are moving to Atlanta, me, Sarai, and Zy'riah...Sarai's firm is putting her in charge of their new Atlanta office. So, she is the reason why we're leaving, not me."

Again silence. "Wait a minute, wait a minute...you mean to tell me that Sarai, your *wife,* is willingly moving her family back to the hometown of your mistress? Man I tell you, you young folks are strange. Strange."

"First of all Pops, Toni was not my mistress. Me and Sarai were separated remember. And secondly...yeah you're right it's crazy. I mean, I have questioned her over and over to determine if this is what she wants but you know Sarai, she's always been ambitious and this is the kind of opportunity that she has waited for all of her career. She has to be the one to make this call."

"Well son I'll tell you what. This is a bad idea...a very bad idea. Your family barely survived the last ordeal and here you are talking about heading back to the scene of the crime. What's more important to Sarai...her family or money? If she can't see what a mistake this is...you certainly need to."

"Pops, I can't. If I talk her out of this, she will resent me. More than she already resents me for...Toni."

He stands up and stretches out his legs. "I'm not going to argue with you son...I hate to see you go...but all I can say is, do what you think is best. Your family, your wife, your daughter...they are your first priority. Good luck telling your mama though. She is going to have a fit when she finds out you're taking her baby."

Our laughter brings the conversation to an uneasy truce. I'm grateful for it. The initial heaviness was beginning to weigh me down. Of course we both know that, although my mom will be upset, my dad will be the one to truly miss Zy'riah. That child is not only her daddy's girl but granddaddy's baby. In fact, even in her young state of mind, she considers him to be her best friend. I hate taking her away from him and them away from her...another difficult element of this situation that has yet to be dealt with.

Just as our conversation comes to a close, I spot my mother's car turning down our street. Bracing myself, I prepare for what is sure to be another long conversation.

*****

Today is the day, and I'm losing my mind about it.

Insane.

Kyle and I are in a better place, yet we have only spoken on the phone. It has been difficult being around him while he is making preparations for Keenan and...Sarai... to arrive. Listening to his conversations with his real estate agent, talking to Keenan...it has been all too surreal...and real. So I've done what I always have... buried myself in my work.

Muse once again has become my sanctuary.

"You've got to be fucking kidding me?" If this wasn't such a serious conversation, Rae's facial expression would be comical. However, this situation is absolutely not a comedy. In fact, it is turning more into a proper Greek tragedy.

"Yep...you heard it."

I begged her to come to Muse today so that I could vent about the new developments in my life. Mr. Jackson is moving back to Atlanta and my world is about to be once again spinning on its axis.

After Keenan's call, I took my time getting out of the shower....needing those extra minutes to get myself together. I knew that he and Kyle still communicated, granted, nothing like they used to. Usually though, I've been lucky enough to not be around when he has actually called. Hearing his name aloud...knowing that on the other end was his smooth voice, was more than my emotions could handle. It had been months since I'd heard his voice...his laugh. I missed it. Then, I found myself staring at Kyle as he told me about the nature of the call. Keenan and Sarai were moving to Atlanta. Not visiting...*moving*...coming to once again invade my own city...on a permanent basis.

Surely life could not be this cruel.

The mere thought of seeing Keenan was difficult to handle. The idea of seeing *them* together...as the married couple that I had once envisioned for our own life, overwhelmed me. If the sofa would have swallowed me whole in that moment, I would have willingly suffocated.

I tried to sustain a poker face, but I could tell by the look on Kyle's face that I wasn't doing a very good job of concealing my true emotions. He wanted to know how I felt...if there would be a problem. He wanted the truth.

Truth?

He didn't want my truth. He didn't want to hear me say that there very well could be a problem...that I was afraid of seeing Keenan again...afraid that those buried yearnings would resurface....that I was afraid that the lies I had been telling myself for months would fracture and reveal hidden truths...that my façade of hate would crumble into a million pieces.

He didn't want that truth no matter how much he convinced himself that he did. So I said nothing...which in hindsight was probably worse, because in that moment, I didn't choose him. I hesitated, even after everything that we have been through: the promises, the new beginnings...the formulation of a new bond of trust. When it came time for me to show up, to speak up...I didn't definitively choose him.

The hurt on his face was obvious as he stood up and silently walked down the hall. I sat immobile on the sofa for what seemed like hours...unsure of how to proceed with this new information. The day was ruined. We never called the crew for a fun night out. Kyle eventually put in unnecessary work on some files while I aimlessly listened to music and watched television. Few words were spoken throughout the rest of the night. When we finally went to bed we stayed on opposite ends. I wanted to retract my silence...to tell him that I loved him and would remain loyal. I wanted to tell him that but the moment had passed and we just had to figure out how to get beyond it. At some point this man was not going to forgive me for my transgressions.

So this morning I woke up and hurried to Muse much earlier than expected. My first order of business was to call Rae. Now here she is, equally confused and bewildered.

"Friend," she states, shaking her head back and forth in an apparent daze. "I would not pay to be you for anything in the world. This is about to be a colossal mess."

"I know Rae" I get up to refresh my coffee. Thankfully there are few customers to interrupt us.

"I mean, how do you feel? What is going through your mind right now? How does Kyle feel? God, there's just so...much."

"I don't know...I will be a complete liar if I say that having Keenan so close will not pose a problem. As much as I want to hate him for what he did, there's still a part of me that carries love for him. All of that...means nothing. We can't be with each other. He's married and now I'm with his best friend...his cousin. There's no coming back from that."

"Ok I hate to be the one to say I told you so...but you know I told your ass so. I said 'do Kyle a favor and make sure you're completely over Keenan before you opt to be in a relationship with him.' It's not fair for him if you still love Keenan. It's just not fair Toni."

Everything about her words makes sense. Fairness, though, is all a matter of perspective. Love...love is a matter of perspective.

"That's the thing Rae...I'm not sure I'll ever be completely over him. So what was I supposed to do...never love again until I detoxed him out of my system. That could've taken a lifetime! All I know is that I was ready...ready to move forward and love a man who I knew was willing and ready to love me back. You can't blame me for wanting that. I was broken Rae." I choked on the words. "I needed that." All of the pain that I have been holding at bay over the past months now threatened to resurface. I can't believe this is happening. Not now, when I am moving forward and making progress.

Rae slouches in her seat and crosses her arms in front of her.

"You still need him Toni. Kyle is your best thing. We all denied it for a long time...but that man loves you. He has been faithful, and kind, and loyal to you. You have got to find a way to let go of Keenan and love him back like he deserves. Let that man go."

I did Rae, I want so desperately to tell her. The question is did *he* free *me?*

*****

There's so much going on in my head right now. My emotions are all over the place. Just when life finally seems to be settling down...this interruption comes out of nowhere.

I really don't know how to feel. On one hand, I miss my cousin. Keenan and I have always been close...more like brothers since both of us were our moms' only kids. I would never think there could be a point in our lives where we weren't communicating. Yet, here we are. The irony of it all is that I'm technically the person to set the wheels in motion.

I was the one who insisted that Keenan move to Atlanta. He and Sarai were in such a bad place that I felt, at least at the time, that he could use the break. And part of me was being selfish. Losing my mom was the worst event of my life. In that moment, I needed a little piece of home. I never thought about having him here...close to Toni. *Until it was too late.*

I should have known better. If my head was in the right place then I would have known better. I know the two of them better than anyone else. I knew that she could love him...a free spirit, artistic soul. Reflecting back, I can only laugh at my naïve foolishness. How often had I wanted them to meet? How many conversations had I spent discussing one with the other? Maybe if they had felt more like strangers then events wouldn't have unfolded as they did. Nevertheless, I can't linger on the "what ifs". The facts are as they are. They met...and they fell in love.

I thought I had lost her, which would have broken my heart. For years I have been in love with Toni but there were so many obstacles keeping me from telling her. For one, she was my best friend and one of the many life lessons that I have learned is that friendship and relationships don't often mix and she was too important for me to lose. So I never said a word. Not through all those years in college when I painstakingly watched her fall in and out of love, not through the broken hearts, not through the Greg fiasco. I just...wasn't ready. I wasn't ready to lose her...wasn't ready period.

After college was law school...after law school was busting my ass trying to climb the corporate ladder. It took long hours, personal sacrifices, and an abundance of prayer to get to where I am now. Blindly, I was ruled by my ambitions and I made my career my ultimate focus.

I never planned on Keenan.

How could I? Fate, sometimes, intervenes in mysterious ways.

Once I realized the situation, I should have let go. That would have been the right thing to do. Yet, I just couldn't. It's not that I didn't know. I knew damn well that Keenan still loved Toni even though he went back to Sarai. Well, Zy'riah. At the end of the day I know he went back for Zy'riah. That's what worries me. That simple fact: he went back out of a sense of duty to his daughter and not because he was still in love with Sarai.

I miss him. Aside from that, I don't want him in Atlanta.

Especially knowing, or at least strongly suspecting, that he still has love for her. And I would be foolish not to be worried about her falling back in love with him. Truthfully, I know that she's never fallen out of love with him. Sometimes I catch her, staring blankly into space...lost deep in her own thoughts. She doesn't say it, but I know...my gut knows... that she is thinking of him. I know when we make love that she is holding back. There is a part of her that I'm just not reaching. Still, I want her too much to concede defeat.

All I can do is just wait patiently and pray that time eases the pain that he has left and the old wounds are scarred over. Time...exactly what I need, for old whispers to silence and old memories to fade into oblivion.

I'll wait; nevertheless, in the back of mind, seeds of doubt still remain.

Chapter 7: Descent

It's been a tough month but the day has arrived for us to move forward with our new life. I have to admit, I'm excited...scared, but excited. Having the opportunity to run my own office is something I have dreamed about since starting at The Paul Agency. I've always been motivated by my ambition. It's what drives me. I never could have dreamed that it would be under these strange circumstances, but, it is what it is.

Not unexpected, my mom went ballistic when I told her about the move. She had diligently convinced me to fight for my husband, only to have me defy logic and drag his ass back to enemy territory. It sounds crazy, I'll admit that; but life is crazy...love, even crazier. This is my life and I refuse to allow another woman the power to dictate how it's operated. I know Keenan still cares for her...hell he may even love her. Regardless...she did not win. He came home. The only issue is whether she will come for him once she knows he's back in town. If she does come, she will have a problem.

Of course I have to wonder about Keenan. Will he reach out to her? Will being in the same city be too much of a temptation?

Only time will tell.

Since Zy'riah is still in school, Keenan's parents have graciously agreed to keep her until we are settled in Atlanta. The last thing I want is to leave my baby girl, yet, we both agree that it isn't fair to uproot her since the school year has already started. Besides, I know she's in good hands. She absolutely adores her grandparents and they in turn adore her. Hopefully they won't spoil her too much in our absence.

Having her stay with my mom was not even an option. Even, now, at the age of sixty, she's still a workaholic. My sense of ambition is truly derived from her gene pool. The only difference is, she eventually sacrificed her marriage for her career, which at times, I sense she regrets. I won't do that. No, I am determined to have it all.

We're expected to arrive in Atlanta shortly after noon. Kyle will pick us up from the airport and the plan is to stay with him until we are able to find a place to rent. Mr. Dependable has already lined up three places for us to view with his real estate agent.

Bright and early Monday morning I will meet Marcus at our new location. He's been in Atlanta for two weeks now making sure everything is set up for the grand opening. The plan is for him to be there for at least six months to help me build a team, then, he will officially turn the reins over to me. I'm ready to hit the ground running...determined to prove my worth.

At the agency's expense, we've hired a driver to take us to the airport. Keenan has been noticeably silent during the ride. In fact, during the past few weeks, he has been unusually somber. Although he's been responding to my initiation of small talk, I can tell that he's really not present. I don't know if it's because the reality of the move has hit home or it's the moment of seeing Kyle again. It's apparent that their estranged status has taken a mental toll on him. I've tried to talk to him about it, although even on his best days, he's not always the most open person.

The entire "situation" leaves me disappointed in him in more ways than one. Keenan should have known better. He should have known there would be sacrifices. There was no way for that situation to turn out good. Instead, like most men, he was thinking with his dick instead of his brain.

"What's on your mind love?"

He smiles wearily, leaning his head back against the plush headrest. "Nothing much...just tired. Glad to at least have this part over and done with."

"I agree. In a few months everything will settle down though. You know I haven't told you often enough how much I appreciate you for making this move. Please don't think for one minute that I don't get the sacrifice you're making."

Silence.

Sometimes getting him to show emotion can be like pulling teeth. After a few minutes he responds "Yeah. I just hope you know what you're doing Sarai. I hope in the end, this...will all be worth everything you're fighting to achieve."

I stare at him blankly, unsure of how to proceed. "Are you saying that I have a reason to be worried?" I search his face for some type of reaction. His feelings of uncertainty are very apparent.

"No Sarai. You don't. I chose you...I chose my family and that's not going to change. All of the reasons why I chose this life...they're still the same."

"Hmmm...ok"

"Besides, if you have any questions, any doubts...why would you ask me to move?"

"Because Keenan...this is what *I* want. Atlanta? Not at all...but this opportunity is what I want...what we need."

"Ok" he concedes. We'll make it work."

I leaned over to kiss him slightly on the lips. It feels good when he responds by pulling me close. I close my eyes as he caresses my face with his fingers. Even with all of our issues I'm still very much attracted to him. That hasn't changed since our days long-ago on Howard's campus. Even then, there was always something special...something...about the way my body responded to his touch. To think that he was with someone else...some other woman... loving her even remotely how he has loved me has torn me to pieces.

I pull away. "How do you feel about seeing Kyle?"

A forceful breath escapes his lips. "I don't know. I guess I'm just glad that we will finally get a chance to talk and clear the air. Maybe begin to get back some type of relationship. I mean we're not just friends but family so at some point we have to communicate."

Now that he is talking I decide to push my luck. "How do you feel about him and...Toni? Being in Atlanta is one thing. Seeing them together...that's a completely different issue. Are you good with that?"

He stares at me for a long time. I hold my breath. I'm not crazy, even though from outside appearances it would seem that I am just that. I know, in spite of what he says, seeing her will be the ultimate test of his faith. Still, we have to take that walk if we're going to truly move forward. If he can't handle this...then he never let her go in the first place.

"Sarai, we are literally on our way to the airport. Are you seriously asking me that now?"

The first stirrings of anger course through my body. I didn't start this conversation to have it end in a fight.

"Keenan, it shouldn't matter when I ask or where...if there is no problem, the answer should always be 'yes'. So, I ask you again...are you good with this?"

Instead of answering, he turns away and stares vacantly out of the car window. Just like that the mood has changed. His body, now taut with tension...his jaw set with frustration.

Without turning my way he simply states, "It's complicated."

Complicated? I can only shake my head. Ok, Keenan, I think to myself. Only time will tell just how complicated this really is.

My own frustration threatens to get the best of me. There is obviously more that he isn't saying; however, I am wise enough to know that I have pushed him enough for one night. Besides, in a few short hours we will make our descent into Atlanta and the life that he had once created in my absence will be revealed.

I turn towards my own window, away from the coldness that now occupies its own space in the car...once again the barrier of that invisible wall...impenetrable.

Chapter 8: Reminisce

Here we are...casually lounging in my house, as if life, for all of us, has not drastically turned upside down. The three of us...valiantly trying to make small talk out of mundane subjects. Not one of us willing to scratch the surface of lingering issues. Crazy...it used to be so easy back in the day when we were young and dumb and full of dreams.

By Keenan's sophomore year in college he and Sarai were practically inseparable. It was strange coming home on breaks and not having my boy all to myself. More times than not, it was the three of us hanging out together, other than those occasions when I dragged along some random chick. In the beginning, I was jealous of their relationship; however, over time, Sarai became more like a sister. I came to love her and the bond that she and Keenan shared. It was good seeing him in love and loved. He deserved it.

What a difference a year makes.

At least Toni isn't here. We respectfully agreed that she will not stay at the house while Keenan and Sarai are here. At some point we will have to come up with a plan on how to integrate our lives. There is no way to truly avoid it. If they are going to be permanent residents of Atlanta, then they will just have to get used to the idea of me and Toni being together.

I dutifully prepare wine and snacks to take out to the pool where they are both chillin...waiting on my imminent return. At least this is a much different atmosphere from the last time that Sarai graced my home with her presence. When she flew in from D.C., fought the valiant fight for her husband, and subsequently altered that state of our lives.

Both of them have already showered and changed into comfortable clothes, Sarai into a yellow maxi dress and Keenan into khaki shorts and a plain white tee. In her absence, I sometimes forget just how beautiful Sarai is. Her long slim legs are stretched out in front of her. Her peach colored skin already glowing from being kissed by the warm southern sun. Since our last encounter, she has dyed her hair a deep hue of red, which would have been gaudy on anyone else. Against her golden complexion it is perfection. Gotta hand it to Keenan...he's certainly one lucky guy. I just hope that one day he actually realizes it.

"About damn time man. What took you so long?" Sarai complains, sitting up to take a chilled glass from the tray.

"Really? You've only been in my house a few hours and you're already complaining? Some people are just ungrateful." I playfully respond. Now it really is beginning to feel like old times. Keenan also takes a glass and it does not go unnoticed how he almost finishes it in one long swig.

Sarai, bossy as normal, takes the lead. "So what's the plan Kyle? It is not my intention to be camped out in your house forever so I really hope your person has come through with some nice places for us to view."

"Trust me. I love you and all but the last thing I want is for you to be a long-term fixture in my household. My real estate agent, Pam, is one of the best in the business so you're definitely in good hands. She was amazing when it came to getting me this house and negotiating the price that I wanted so no worries, she will get you what you're looking for."

"Music to my ears." She grabs a handful of grapes and methodically eats them one by one. "You know Kyle I appreciate you for doing this. With everything that has happened, the last thing I want to do is inconvenience you in any way. This will definitely be challenging but we're going to work this out. I know you already have your 'friends' here but my expectation is that you will be just as involved in our lives. I want Zy'riah to have time to really get to know her Uncle Kyle. Ok?"

My eyes wander to Keenan who is staring vacantly out at the pool. It's more than evident that he wants no part of this conversation. Even so, it is here and I don't see any reason to dismiss it.

"Me too Sarai. I want us all to be closer. I've missed seeing you guys, hanging out. Let's be real though...all of this...it will take time. I can't see this interaction happening any time soon. How does this work, having everyone in the same space? The same events? You don't think the wounds are still too ...fresh?"

There's instant fire in her eyes. "Of course we can't exist in the same space. That's certainly not my intent. Just because I moved to *her* city does not mean that I'm giving that woman an all access pass to my husband. I just know that in order for this to work for you two," she glares at me and Keenan, "...there will be times when I will have to tolerate her."

"What about you?" The question is for Keenan who continues to remain stoic and distant.

"What do you mean?" he feigns ignorance, although he knows that I'm not fooled. He knows exactly what I mean. This is the first time that I get to confront him face to face...man to man. I need an answer while I can look him in the eye, watch his body signals and know where he stands when it comes to Toni. I don't care that Sarai has to witness the exchange.

He looks at Sarai, who is watching him closely. Obviously the move, or Toni at least, is an unresolved issue between them. Witnessing their exchange, or lack thereof, frustrates the hell out of me. Ever since I've known Sarai she's been ambitious. She's worked harder, longer, faster than anyone else, always trying to stay one step ahead of the competition. Being in the rat race myself, I've understood it, and I've always admired her for it. Still, this...this is a foolish move. Now that the deed is done, I just hope that her blind ambition hasn't doomed us all.

Keenan drains his glass and finally speaks. "Am I ok with being back here...am I ok with you two being...together? Nah, I'm not...but I wish you well. I just want to move forward with my life. That's all."

"Well then that settles it." Sarai responds, her voice oddly cold. She never takes her eyes off of Keenan as she raises her glass. When she speaks next, every single word drips with sarcasm.

"Here's to moving on."

*****

Our conversation continues well into the night. We order food, listen to music...reminisce about the good 'ole days at Howard. It's nearly two in the morning, when Sarai goes to bed...she has an early meeting with Marcus in the morning. That leaves me and Keenan in silence...nursing beers, each not wanting to disrupt the mood with conversations we are both too exhausted to face.

At some point, I brave the question that I hope can give me great insight into his frame of mind.

"Tell me something Keenan. Are you happy with the choice you made?"

He leans back on the sofa, a hopeless look of defeat planted firmly on his face.

"It doesn't matter my brother...it's already done."

Chapter 9: At First Sight

After weeks of preparation, The Paul Agency is ready for its official grand opening. Marcus and I have put in long hours to make sure that it goes off without a hitch. We have even managed to hire an office manager and sometime in the near future, we'll be in the hunt for a part-time intern and another associate. Atlanta's professional pool of graduates should prove ripe for the picking.

There is at least another hour before the doors officially open but already, a line of people are waiting in the lobby. Marcus has spared no expense in making this a true- to- life red carpet event. There are photographers, bloggers, athletes, entertainers...a compiled list of Atlanta's elitist and finest. He reached deep into the recesses of his black book to invite guests he had at some point encountered in his professional career as a former pro athlete and since opening the D.C office. There is a DJ, expensive food, and an abundance of alcohol. Even beyond the stress and the nervousness, the excitement of the night settles in.

My season has arrived.

In measured taste, I ensure that am styled for the role. My strapless black cocktail dress caresses my slim form and perfectly complements my freshly dyed deep red hair. My hair, the perfect complement to my glowing peach skin tone. When I glanced at my reflection in the mirror before leaving, I saw a boss chick, one who has it all together. It's exactly what I'm aiming for.

My reality, however, is just short of turmoil. Keenan and I have recently moved into a spacious townhouse in Dunwoody, not far from the location of the office. I am glad not to be living with Kyle anymore. Although I'm grateful for all of his help with our relocation, I can't help feeling some kind of way about him "dating" or whatever the hell he's doing with Toni. Keenan and Kyle may have their issues but there's no way around seeing him, socializing with him...now that we're all back in the same city. With him being with Toni, that mean there's no way around seeing her...having her unwillingly pulled into my...our circle.

I've been trying to gauge Keenan's thoughts but his moods have become increasingly difficult to read. Is he thinking of her? Is there some invisible pull of gravity taking place before my eyes...stronger now with proximity? I can't figure it out. All I can hope is that "this" settles down and we can get back to the business of living our normal lives.

As if my thoughts alone somehow magically conjure him up, he strolls through the door. My breath catches in my throat. The hidden anger and disappointment cannot mask the fact that my husband is a beautiful man. His dreads are pulled back into a sleek, tamed bun. The suit I had specifically tailored for him, perfectly accents his toned frame. Even without being considered tall, he carries such a presence. With subtle confidence, he walks towards me and out of my peripheral vision I witness Tammi, our new office manager, eyeing him. Yes, tonight I am proud to call him mine.

When he approaches I give him a slight hug and an air kiss, careful not to tarnish my professionally applied make-up. He pulls back and his eyes roam longingly over my body. It's been a long time since I've seen that special look in his eye. Just maybe there's hope for us after all.

"Sarai you are stunning." The sincerity of the compliment causes me to blush.

"You're looking pretty gorgeous yourself husband."

I reach out to grab his hand, linking my manicured fingers through his. The past weeks have been a struggle, but I think it's important for him to know that I'm still in the fight.

"I'm proud of you baby. You deserve every bit of success that comes your way."

My emotions spin with the weight of his words. There are moments when he, the only man I have ever loved, can still have this impact on me. "Thank you," I whisper looking up at his handsome face. "That means more to me than you know."

For a time we stand like two awkward teenagers, grinning at each other for no apparent reason. Then we laugh and the spell is broken.

"Come on." I lead him towards the front of the room. "The people are waiting." I can't resist winking at Tammi as we pass her way. Yeah I see you looking.

We find Marcus, who is already giving interviews to select press. When he sees me he immediately calls me over. With regret, I leave Keenan's side to fulfill my hosting duties. When Marcus finishes, we do exactly as he always envisioned...walk out as power team making it known that we were here in Atlanta not only to play...but to win.

The standard red ribbon is cut and Marcus gives a brief speech before the crowd is formally ushered into the suite of offices. As I get caught up in the whirlwind of guests, Keenan is unfortunately left to his own devices. For a good hour, Marcus keeps me on my toes, making sure to introduce me to all on the list of "those to know" and possible future clients. As we wrap up a conversation with one of the many artists on the scene, I catch a glimpse of a Kyle at the front entrance. Before I can fully register his presence, there is another familiar face that steals my attention. She wears a strapless red dress that clings to her curves like a second skin. Her hair hangs in loose, natural spirals around her shoulders. Even being small in stature, she garners tons of attention as she enters the room.

Toni.

Instinctively, I search the crowd for Keenan. I easily spot him at the bar. Tammi is by his side, chatting incessantly, but it is painfully clear that he is not paying attention to a word she is saying. Instead, his eyes are transfixed on the door.

As always his emotions are hard to read. Still, there is no mistaking the clenched jaw...the lined forehead. My gaze wanders back to her and even though she is with one of the most eligible bachelors in the city, it is easy to see that her attention is solely focused on someone else.

My husband.

She is not as successful as Keenan at hiding her emotions. She appears...pained. As pained as he is clearly distressed.

Without notice, I abandon Marcus and rapidly make my way across the room. He is so focused on his prior mistress that he isn't even aware of my presence...until I snake my arm through his. I reach up to guide his face toward mine.

"Are we good?" I ask, hating the fact that I need this reassurance. He stares at me blankly for a minute before turning back towards the door. A long sigh escapes his beautiful lips.

"Yes Sarai, we are good."

Arm in arm we turn to greet our new guests. It takes less than two minutes before I am once again face to face with the woman who slept with my husband...who made him fall in love with her.

"Sarai...Keenan." It is Kyle who is the first to speak. "This is quite the turnout. You two look amazing."

"Thank you sweetheart," I respond, leaning in to kiss his cheek. "I'm glad our hard work over the past few weeks seems to be paying off."

I turn to face her then.

"Toni."

With unflinching pride, she stares back at me.

"Sarai."

Then, casually dismissing me, she turns to face him. "Hello Keenan...it's good to see you again." Even though she is making a valiant attempt to be pleasant, her voice is clearly strained.

"It's good to see you too Toni. Both of you...actually."

"Really?" She has the audacity to ask with a smirk on her face.

"Yes...really."

"Well isn't this lovely...old friends getting together to catch up." I'm sure the sarcasm is evident in my voice. As we stand for a moment in awkward silence a waiter walks past with a tray of champagne. We all reached out simultaneously to stop her. I desperately search for an excuse to bolt when Keenan, on his own accord, expands the conversation.

"So...how are Rae and Dawn?" The question is directed at Toni.

"Good actually, Dawn was going to come but Lexie wasn't feeling well and Jamie had to work. You know...well," she looks helplessly towards Kyle, "maybe you don't know...she and Jamie are back together."

"Really" he states, clearly caught off guard by that news. "Wow. After everything Dawn went through with him, I have to say that I'm surprised."

"Yeah we were too. I guess it's been the season for second chances."

Whether intentional or not, the ill-timed joke falls flat. I can't stomach being in her presence, but I won't dare leave Keenan. I squeeze his arm, hoping he gets the hint. Instead, he continues with his inquisition.

"Rae?"

This time Kyle answers. "Rae will definitely be here tonight. Of course her boss is asking the associates to come so they can stake out the competition."

Competition? Maybe for now as we're just planting our seeds. There is no doubt in my mind however, that once I get the agency firmly established, there will be no competition to speak of.

"And exactly who is...Rae?" My tone is deliberately condescending.

"My best friend." Toni answers defensively.

"I see." Again the awkwardness settles in. Incapable of bearing the forced camaraderie any longer, I back away, pulling Keenan with me.

"Well, as lovely as this is, I have some people that I need for *my husband* to meet. Please...mingle, eat, drink."

I walk off without further words. Tonight is my night and I refuse to spend any more of the evening sharing it with *her.* As we walk away I lean in towards Keenan. I know he says that he is good; still, there is an uneasy feeling of doubt settling into the pit of my belly. Sensing my mood, he wraps his arms around me and plants a firm kiss on the top of my head.

This for now will do.

*****

The mere thought of attending the open house tonight for The Paul Agency has my anxiety level on ten. Truthfully, I would rather be anywhere else in the world; however, there is no good way or reason to explain the why's of it all to Kyle. He wants to go...needs to go, professionally and personally. He feels the need to support Keenan and Sarai. Also, being a young professional in Atlanta, he won't miss out on a great opportunity to network and socialize. In this city, the premise of success starts with the foundation of being seen.

While I should be thinking on the same level, for Muse's sake at least, the last thing I'm concerned about is business. I just want to focus on surviving the night. So I put on my big girl panties and prepare myself for what is to come. Needless to say, my preparation is not sufficient.

Kyle and I are in complete silence on the ride over. I don't think either of us is in the mood for false pretenses. We both understand the significance of this event. I pray that I can pass the test. Yet, all hopes vanish the moment I step through the doors and see him.

Beautiful him.

One year. It has been one long, devastating year, since the last time I saw him. In this moment though, my heart doesn't recognize the time. It is beating just as furiously as it did during those months when we were familiar. My body instantly reacts as if there was not a gap in time or distance. And that saddens me...because it is in this moment that I realize that I still love him. Even with all of the lies, the misunderstandings, the hurt, and so much of the pain...I love him.

There is a sea of bodies between us, yet our eyes somehow find each other. Across the room, a silent conversation commences. *Hey you*...we seem to say in our own familiar language. Because I see it...a tiny bit of reaction. It is spoken in the set of his jaw, the tenseness of his face. All of the telling signs which indicate that he is distressed...and if he is distressed, then he is feeling some kind of way about seeing me too.

I turn my focus towards Kyle as I feel his hand slip into my own. "You good?" he asks. Before I respond, I glance back at Keenan once more and see Sarai, beautiful Sarai, as she intertwines her arms with his.

His wife...her husband.

"Yes...I'm good."

The smile he gives me is worth the lie. He raises one eyebrow in that charming way of his. "So shall we get this over with?" I sigh and allow him to lead us right into the midst of the enemy's circle.

*****

This small talk is killing me. I'm finding it increasingly difficult to be cordial when there are still so many underlying questions. This is not only my first time seeing Keenan but actually witnessing him and Sarai together. It pains me to admit it, but they are a stunning couple. She, of course, takes full advantage of the opportunity to rub it all in. Throughout the meaningless conversation, she flirtatiously leans into his shoulder, squeezes his hand, whispers in his ear. I die a little bit with each emotional display. Still, I keep my poker face intact, even though internally I am coming undone. Thankfully, her boss, Marcus, I think, calls her over and the ordeal is finally over. I have faced my demons and lo and behold, I am still standing. Somehow that small victory does little to assuage my turmoil.

We mingle for another hour before I feign exhaustion and beg Kyle to leave. I'd hoped to catch Rae so I could at least have a friendly face in the midst, but she never arrives. He is not fooled, aware of the real issue; however, in true Kyle fashion, he doesn't mention anything. He says his goodbyes, exchanges last minute pleasantries and we leave...the silence once again our traveling companion.

Automatically, and without question, he drives to his home, a welcome option now that his guests have moved out. Sensing my mood he goes to the kitchen and pours two glasses of wine. I finish mine with ease. Before there is any conversation he kisses me...hard, deep. Somewhere in that kiss is the desperation of a man who doesn't want to lose. It is so intense that I feel shockwaves throughout my entire body. I kiss him back with equal passion, desperate to cling to the reality of our life together....desperately trying to erase the memories of long-lost moments.

We cling to each other in a state of raw emotions and passions. When he finally pulls away, I can feel my mouth swelling from the brutal attack. I don't care. I need him. I have always needed him. Deftly he wraps his fingers around my now disheveled hair while his other hand goes to work removing my dress. I try in vain to remove his clothing but my fingers are shaking too bad to be much of a success. Instead, when he has me in front of him...nude, exposed, he steps back and slowly removes them himself. As he unbuttons, unties, unzips...he never removes his gaze from mine. There is so much love and "want" in his eyes. Tears form in my own as I look away. In this moment I feel so undeserving. How can I not love this man as much as he loves me? He is so willing to give me all of himself while all I long for is the forbidden love of another.

I feel his hands brush against my face. His soft lips kiss away my tears. Again he finds my mouth...pushing, prodding...begging...daring me to let him in. I relent...and give in.

He drags me down with him to the floor; the feel of the soft carpet teases my skin. His long fingers are everywhere, touching, caressing...teasing. I close my eyes...completely giving in to the ecstasy of the moment. I grab his head bringing his hot, wet mouth closer to my aching nipples. He doesn't disappoint, sucking each one as if he a starved man. I cry out, squirming beneath him as his fingers find the folds of my womanhood. In expert fashion he parts my lips, easing his way inside.

"Damn baby" his voice comes in ragged breaths as I leave his fingers drenched in my juices. I wrap my arms around his neck pulling him in closer, harder. We rock together in a synchronized rhythm, his fingers working their magic against my pussy and clit. Just as I am about to explode from pleasure, he pulls out, then immediately fills the void with his engorged penis. I brace myself for his assault but to my surprise he once again wraps his fingers around my hair and remains still. The weight of his head is buried in the folds of my neck. I don't want this stillness. I want him to take me...make me...forget. I move beneath him... trying desperately to entice him into action. After some time, he looks up smiling that gorgeous smile.

"Woman" he starts, his voice husky with hunger. "Will you please stop? I'm trying hard not to lose it."

I grab his face, pulling it towards mine. "Lose it" I whisper as I bite his bottom lip. He groans in agony.

"Stop," he pleas in a hoarse whisper. This time I slowly lick his lips, his neck...his ear. "Lose...it" I once again command. His attempt at resistance is weak...he can't deny me. His grip on my hair tightens as I feel him shift above me.

"Yes baby" I whimper in anticipation. He closes his eyes, relenting to my demands and goes to work. Again and again and again he slow strokes my body causing me to scream his name with wild abandonment. I wrap my arm around his narrow waist, pulling him in deeper and deeper. He doesn't hold back, giving me all of him in long thrusts that seem to fill my entire being. His fingers are wound in my tangled coils, pulling and grabbing at will. The tears that flood my face are a seductive mix of ecstasy and pain. Our naked, drenched bodies soon find their perfect rhythm in this primal dance. Before long his speed increases, and we find ourselves...lost… in the sounds, the smells...the taste, of us.

Together, we explode.

*****

We never make it off of the floor. At some point, Kyle finds a blanket to cover us and we lay...nestled together in our artificial haven until the first rays of the morning sun slither through the partially open blinds.

There is no further conversation about Keenan.

Still...I don't kid myself. The damage has been done. Pandora's Box has been opened allowing Keenan's ghost to escape. I sense his presence hovering in the dark shadows of the night...*waiting*.

Chapter 10: Late Nights

A month passes and the verdict is still out on whether or not I like this city. For years I've heard that Atlanta is the Mecca for Black people. It's the place where we can come and prosper...where we exist, not in the shadows of others, but in the forefront...where we as a people bask in the rays of our own fabricated sun; the very place where the existence of African history is woven through its cultural fabric.

I'm not impressed.

For a city that's been defined by one races' success, it is also one in which not everything is what it seems. Even in the short period of time that I have called it home, I've witnessed the infiltration of a new paradigm...the stain of pop culture, the detriment of social influence. What's left is only a mockery of what once was.

For the past month we have been steadily building our clientele. In a month's time, we have made tremendous progress. Marcus Paul has always been a wise man when it comes to business and he has proven himself once again by choosing this location to expand his brand. This is a city where image is everything...where even its least ones want to be...someone. The doors were opened, the call was put out...they, in turn, have answered.

They have come to us from varying backgrounds but mostly from the field of entertainment...struggling singers, lowly actors, sub-par producers. They all want to enhance their image...or rather to re-create them. Fine by me. Let them come.

Each one, in their own way, further solidifies my success. Makes all of this...worth it.

This, of course, being the move to Atlanta. Admittedly, I've second guessed myself in the past few weeks. Have I allowed my blind ambition to get the best of me? Am I sacrificing my marriage, my family...for a certain level of success? I still don't have the answer, and honestly, I don't have the mental capacity to think it through. My goal is to stay focused. I promised Marcus...made promises to myself...and there is nothing that can keep me from seeing that through.

Not even Keenan.

No, I made that mistake once and I vowed not to do it again. This time...he will need to be the one to step up and keep his promises.

"Sarai, are you ready?"

Breaking out of my trance, I notice Tammi standing in the doorway. Her stealth-like movements always catch me off guard. There's just something unnerving about the way she slinks around the office. Truthfully, if she wasn't so skilled in office management, I wouldn't keep her on. But it's not the time to rock the boat. There is too much yet to be done, and for now she's proven to be an asset.

I glance at the small clock above the doorframe. *Four o'clock.* Somehow the day has gotten away from me. It is time for our daily meeting with Marcus, who is highly involved in that way. Until he is satisfied that business is being conducted exactly as he sees fit, he expects regular reports and updates on clients and potential clients. Tedious, yes...demanding, certainly...still, you can't argue with a man who is well on his way to building an empire.

"Yes," I answer. "Please let Marcus know that I'm on my way." Without another word, she slithers out of the doorway.

I grab my growing stack of files, the nearest pen and pad and head to the conference room, where King Marcus awaits my arrival.

When I enter the room, I can tell by the scowl on his face that he is not pleased with my tardiness.

"Nice of you to join us Ms. Jackson."

Not bothering to acknowledge his statement, I sit opposite of him at the long table. In the beginning, I thought it was strange having such a massive piece of furniture in the room when there are so few employees. Marcus, being a true visionary, instructed me to visualize every chair being occupied by future employees, clients...other important people. His motto, if you "see" it, you can achieve it.

I spread out my files in front of me and smile, preparing for him to start.

We go over the numbers for the month and it's more than obvious that he's impressed. Business is booming and that makes him happy. If Marcus is happy, I am ecstatic.

"Listen ladies," He starts after completing his update. "I want to thank you for the work that you've put into making this branch a success. I know I have pushed you with the long hours and endless calls, but please know that I appreciate you. You should definitely pat yourselves on the backs for a job well done."

His compliments leave me beaming with pride. Putting it all into perspective makes the sacrifices worth it; especially when the numbers speak for themselves.

"Having said that" he continues leaning back in his seat, "I think we should adjust our time frame. At the start of this journey, I was thinking that we wouldn't need to hire additional staff for at least three to six months; however, with the clients that we already have on board and our list of potentials steadily growing, we have to speed up that time-frame. Next week I want to start the process of hiring an associate and maybe even a temp or intern. I'm sure you can use the help on the front end Tammi."

"Absolutely, Mr. Paul." She answers, while I nod in agreement.

This is surprising, albeit good news. I couldn't have imagined being at the point of hiring staff this soon, but getting at least one new associate on board could really tighten operations up. This juggling act between him and I can only last for so long before clients start falling through the cracks.

"So what's the game plan Marcus?" I inquire, knowing that he will want to move as swiftly as possible.

"Well," he glances in Tammi's direction. "I'm thinking that Tammi and I can get a game plan together to pull a list of potential associates, then, you and I can start the interviewing process. I'm hoping to have someone in place within the next two to three weeks. That's a quick turnaround I know, but I have faith that you ladies can make it happen."

"Of course," I easily agree, knowing that I will indeed, get it done.

We go over some general housekeeping before Marcus officially ends the meeting. As I pack up my belongings he signals for me to wait. I abruptly stop and sit back down, checking the time as I do. The long day, another one without much of a break, has left me starving. Hopefully, this impromptu meeting isn't going to take long. As soon as Tammi is out of earshot Marcus turns to face me.

"Look Sarai, I personally want to thank you for the great job you're doing. Without question, I don't think we would be as far along with this office as we are if you weren't involved. We undoubtedly make a great team."

I am taken aback by his words. Marcus is tough...fair, but tough. I've been working my ass off to get this office up and running and I know the numbers certainly reflect that. Still, getting a compliment from him this early in the game is not an easy feat, and certainly not to be taken lightly.

"Thank you Marcus. I appreciate your recognition of my work. I hope you know...or at least you're getting to that point...where you see how serious I am about my career and longevity with your agency."

He stretches out his long, lean legs in front of him. "I do. I see it. I know it can't be easy coming back here with everything that's happened. I genuinely respect the fact that you didn't allow your personal issues to interfere with your career. You made the right decision, at least from my perspective."

Good to know that he was that assured because, in truth, I was beginning to have my doubts. I've been so determined to have it all, yet, there are times when I face myself in the mirror and I'm unsure of exactly what I want. The silence hangs heavy in the air for a minute before he abruptly stands.

"Well, I guess you better get out of here. Thirty more minutes and you will be stagnant in traffic. This rain won't make it any easier."

"What about you?" I ask. "You do realize that you're allowed a break right...that it's actually ok for you to have a life?"

He laughs. "Don't do that Sarai. You, of all people, know that this agency is my life. If I don't get this last report finished, I will think about it all night so I may as well settle in, roll up my sleeves, and get it done."

I check my watch once again. He is absolutely right about the traffic. Even though I promised Keenan tonight wouldn't be a late one, the echo of Marcus' compliments rings fresh in my ears. I can't see leaving him alone with so much work still to be done.

"Thai or soul-food?" I ask.

He stares at me for a minute. "What do you mean?"

"Thai or soul-food sir?" I blatantly repeat the question. "Look, if you're in for the night then I am too."

"You don't have to do this Sarai", he counters. "I'm sure you need to get home to Keenan. I'm ok."

"I know I don't have to Marcus. I *want* to. Like you said...we're a team. Besides, working together, we'll get this done in half of the time. No partner left behind."

He smiles before reluctantly giving in. "Ok."

I call in an order to be delivered. My next call is to Keenan to let him know that I will be working late...again. As predicted, he isn't happy about it but I can't let it concern me. I'm sure he will find some way to occupy his time. After all...this is a city he once called home.

When I think of you, I think of music...the wail of a bass guitar...fingers strumming perfect chords synchronized with poetic words of Love...and sometimes when I think of you...my thoughts are like Dali clocks...time suspended...reminiscent of intimate moments...lost

I think of conversations shared...whispered words of affection in secret nights...I think of when I loved you...when my love was hunger...craving for the taste of you...And in those moments when I think of you...I often wonder...

do you think of me too?

*****

Chapter 11: A Familiar Face

I'm supposed to be at Muse, but I'm late as usual. It seems lately, that all of my bad habits are coming back to haunt me. It's a humid, rainy day, and on rainy days, Atlanta traffic habitually comes to a complete standstill. Even though I've been living here for years, it never ceases to amaze me how something as simple and natural as rain has the power to shut the city down. Already, there are several wrecks causing major delays.

I call Mia to let her know that I'm on the way. She quickly instructs me not to rush since apparently it's been a slow day. Not surprising with the weather the way it is. Actually, other than the inconvenience of traffic, I am glad for the rain. It fits the state of my current mood perfectly. My mind is so clouded with thoughts...thoughts of Kyle, Keenan...Sarai. It is so frustrating to see my life unraveling before my eyes. One man...one man is responsible for causing all of this chaos. Mr. Keenan Jackson just won't leave me in peace.

At last, there is a break in traffic and without further delay, I am able to make it to Muse in less than an hour. By the time I park and enter the building, my hair and clothes are thoroughly drenched. The stark coldness already seems to be seeping into every pore of my being.

Mia is at the counter with our one lone customer who dared venture out in these conditions. Considering how intensely he was looking at her and how she was smiling at him with her bright eyes and dimple on full display, I'm sure there was more behind his motive.

Without interrupting, I head to the back of the office. Because Muse is my second home, I always keep extra clothes, blankets and other necessities on hand; however, the only items that I can seem to locate are gym pants and tank tops. Not exactly business attire, but I'm certain that we won't get many customers out in this weather. In fact, if it continues, I may just decide to close up shop a little early.

By the time I return to the front, the customer has taken residence in a booth in the back corner of the Muse. He looks up only briefly as I pass before returning his attention to some sports magazine that he has collected.

"You know Toni," Mia starts in as I make a bee-line to the carafe of coffee on the front counter. "You really didn't have to come in. It's been dead all day. Leave it to you to brave a freaking storm trying to come into the office when you could be at home curled up on the sofa...or in the bed...with that fine ass man of yours."

The one thing I've come to love about Mia is how forthright and opinionated she is. It has taken her a minute to find her voice but now that she has...she openly speaks her mind.

"Little girl get out of grown folk business and get out of my bedroom. That fine ass man of mine had to work so I was by myself anyway."

Mia rolls her eyes as she follows me to my usual booth. "I'm just saying...here I am single, searching for Mr. Right and you treat your dude as if he's a casual distraction. Just wait...when my man comes through I won't be spending late nights at Muse."

"Girl, stop it. I don't treat Kyle that way. He knows my heart and I know his ambitions...*this* works for us. And from my point of view," I let my gaze travel to the back of the store. "…you seem to have found *something*."

She lets out a small laugh before leaning in close to speak in muted tones. "Yeah, maybe a *lil* something. That's my new "friend" Curt. I met him this weekend at that Exposure Open Mic event I went to with Rae. Isn't he…delicious?"

I secretly glanced over her shoulder to get a better view of the "friend." He was indeed handsome with a caramel complexion and freshly lined, closely cropped beard. He seemed from first appearance at least, more mature and clean cut than the guys Mia usually dates.

"Let's just say that I definitely approve." I smile. "But what the hell happened to Slain, Sloan, whatever his name is."

She balls up her napkin and throws it directly in my face. "You know what Toni, that's not even funny. You know his name was Slay." I know…I just find great joy in teasing her about her tragic love for lost poets.

"What? Girl I can't keep up with your poet of the moment. If you would just leave these starving artists alone you may be able to make room for the 'Curts' you deserve. Not the men that keep whispering those sweet words of nothing in your little ear. That's real talk."

"Honey, you are so right…but lawd they sure do sound good in the midnight hours."

I laugh loudly at her silly ass. Oh to be young and dumb again. Then as I think about it, here I am, allegedly the wiser one, and I still find myself caught up in sweet nothings. Obviously, you are never too old to be a fool.

"Don't I know it."

There is a questioning look on her face.

"What Mia?"

She leans forward on the table towards me, as if she is about to reveal some sort of grand secret. "You know...word on the street is that Mr. Keenan Jackson is back in town."

Atlanta, unfortunately, is a big city that can too often feel very small. Of course she knows. Although I haven't directly provided her that info, I'm sure she's caught on to conversations with or between Dawn and Rae.

"And what does that have to do with me?" I hope the sarcasm lacing my voice is convincing.

"Really Toni...only *everything*. It's no secret that man had you so far gone that you didn't know if you were coming or going...and now he's back? Crazy! How is that supposed to work?"

Yep. She's definitely found her voice, although, at this point, I'm not in any kind of mood to hear anything about Keenan....nothing past or present.

"First of all, you don't know what kind of impact that man had on me because I didn't tell you my business. Secondly, I am far removed from anything and everything related to Keenan Jackson so where he is, is certainly no concern of mine."

I try my best to speak with conviction; however, I can tell from Mia's face that she clearly isn't buying anything that I am attempting to sell about my "situation" with Keenan.

"Yeah ok, whatever you say. I'm just glad that I'm working here full-time now so that I can witness all of the dramatics. I may be young, but don't get it twisted, I am far from foolish. That man...is trouble waiting to happen."

Without bothering to acknowledge her bleak premonition, I take a long sip of my coffee. Her statement is all truth. On the very first night I met Keenan, I knew that he would be trouble. I felt it to the very core of my being, even as temptation blinded me. In hindsight, I should have paid more attention to my inner voice because, after all was said and done, he more than exceeded that expectation.

Mia senses the change in my mood and graciously deflects the conversation. "Well...anyway...you want to hear about my weekend?" She sneaks a look at Curt then back to me. The devious look on her face lets me know that I'm in for an earful.

"Of course Mia, how can I resist your little fast ass."

Our conversation lasts for about an hour and in that time, no other customers come in. I had high hopes that the rain would let up, but the downpour remained brutal. If it continues like this then I definitely won't keep the store open the entire night. In fact, I will probably send Mia home early and crash on the sofa in the back.

As much as I love busy days...business equates to money...there is bliss to be found in days like this. The warm colors of Muse, along with the dim lights, make for a cozy, intimate atmosphere. A generic soundtrack has been opted out in favor of my iPod playlist. Currently, Marsha Ambrosius' sexy voice on "Late Night, Early Mornings" is making me wish that I had convinced Kyle to stay at home with me after all.

"Mia, honestly you can take off anytime you want. Unless you just want to hang around to get some extra hours. I don't think anything more is happening around here tonight."

"Seriously?" She could barely contain her excitement. "I mean normally I would stay but I can really think of better things I could be doing in this weather." Her response is accompanied by a sneaky smirk on her face.

"You know what...get out of here with your grown self."

We both laugh as she starts hastily gathering her belongings. It's hard to believe that she was once timid and naïve with her now being this grown woman in the throes of discovering her sexuality. She's become quite comfortable in her own skin.

I remember those days...when life, relationships, sex...was much less complicated.

Within twenty minutes she and Curt are rushing out of the door.

"Bye Curt...enjoy the night," I tease as I get up to close the door behind them. He smiles a beautiful smile in response as Mia makes it a point to roll her eyes before they fully disappear into the darkness.

It's early in the evening, but the presence of dark gray clouds indicates a much later time. I lock the door but at the last minute, I decide against putting up the "CLOSED sign...just in case. That done I settle in, close my eyes and lose myself in the sultry music floating throughout the empty space.

A soft knock on the glass interrupts my trance. I couldn't believe another soul braved this god-forsaken weather.

The sight of the familiar face staring back at me jars my soul. In an instant, I am overcome by an onslaught of conflicting emotions...hate, anger, lust...love...then hate again. I am transported back to the first time he came to Muse and I allowed him entrance into my world. His very presence proved to be a disruptive force of nature. I didn't know...I didn't know then what it would come to be. Now, things are different. I am fully aware of the chaos he leaves in his wake.

Yet...even in the heightened midst of my anger, I find myself wanting to let him in. Even now, his magnetic pull deems me powerless. I can't breathe. Without warning, the tears come, which frustrates me even more. Who is he to do this? He doesn't get to come back into my life knowing how he walked out of it.

Against my own inhibitions, I storm across the room...each step decreasing the distance between us, until... there is only the barrier of the door and the glass separating our bodies. My head screams to keep this door closed but my heart wants to let him in...wants to once again have him in my world, even if for a brief moment. I open the door and back away... allowing 5'8, 180 lbs. of chocolate goodness to walk into the door. His hair is pulled back into a band. Even constrained, I can tell that his dreads are longer. His skin...even smoother than I recalled in my dreams. No more than two minutes have passed and already things are...changed.

I want to yell at him...scream all of the obscene words I have stored in my brain over the past year, but…he is so damn beautiful that my voice only manages to escape my breath in a pained whisper.

"Why are you here?"

His mouth opens, yet no words come out. From the wariness in his eyes, I can tell that he is second-guessing this decision.

"Why are you here?" Louder, more forceful. In the presence of his weakness I find myself gaining strength.

"I don't know Toni." At last he speaks. "I don't know. I just...needed to see you."

"See me?" He can't be serious. "What good does it do for you to come see me? If you're going to have the audacity to come see me you better have the courage not to hide. Are you really ready to *see* all of me Keenan? See my pain. See the woman whose heart you tore into shreds. Do you see that? Do you see the wounds that are still here? Do you see what you have done by coming back here?"

I wait for him to cower away. Instead, there is a reaction that catches me completely off guard.

Tears.

I've never seen him cry. Emotional, yes...pained, absolutely...never though, have I seen him cry.

Until now.

In this moment I am fully aware of his motive. He may have chosen her...but he still wants me.

Damn.

*****

The sting of bourbon burns my throat but serves its purpose of awakening my senses. The house is quiet... the night is dark and still.

Too still.

Quietude has never been my friend...it provides too much opportunity for me to get lost in the throes of tortuous thoughts. Thoughts that should be forbidden, but they come, nevertheless. Thoughts of wild hair, pretty brown skin, soulful eyes.

Toni.

Now that I've seen her...had the luxury of holding her in my arms again, I can't forget her. I thought I was prepared, but I should have known better. The moment I saw her walk through the doors of The Paul Agency, I knew I was in trouble.

I tried in vain to keep my emotions in check. I couldn't let Sarai in on my distress, my pain. Yet when our eyes found each other, I knew that *she* knew. There we were, in a room of a hundred people...and she was all that I could see.

I didn't expect the pain. Ever since I found out about her and Kyle, I had steeled myself against any and all feelings related to her. Had to...or it would have driven me insane thinking about him loving her....him kissing her. Still, when she stepped into the room I couldn't deny my feelings. Her petite form was molded into her dress. Her unruly hair cascaded in wondrous coils around her beautiful face. In a single moment, I wanted to kiss her perfectly glossed lips...wanted to caress her silky, earth toned flesh...wanted to smell the scent of her favorite perfume that I imagined lingered on her skin. I wanted so badly to hear her husky voice whisper words of affection in my ear. *I missed her.* And seeing her made me realize that I wanted her all over again.

Then, another familiar face appeared by her side, stealing the attention that I longingly craved.

Kyle.

His presence was a bold reminder that she no longer belonged to me...that my claim to her expired the moment that I went home.

I sensed Sarai's presence even before I felt her arms loop through my own.

Claiming me.

I turned my attention to my wife, the woman I had chosen. When I told her I was good, I meant it. It wasn't until later, as I sat on our balcony, drinking by myself under the cloak of darkness, that I realized that I would never be good. Not as long as Toni was with someone else...especially my cousin...my best friend. It was then that I decided that I would go to her.

Damn, only a few weeks into my new life and I was already flailing.

I knew she would be angry. We hadn't officially spoken since the day I left. Well, we had that one random conversation but that was about it other than a few non-committal texts. I could only imagine how she was feeling now that I was back. I should have called her....even before I called Kyle. However, I wasn't prepared to hear her voice. I was too much of a coward for that.

The storm provided me with a grand opportunity. Sarai stayed late at the office to catch up on some work, while waiting for the roads to clear up. I envisioned Toni sitting at her favorite booth in Muse, sipping her beloved coffee. I tortured myself trying to guess her mood. Would she choose the sweetness of caramel macchiato or was she in the mood for the silky texture of a dark chocolate mocha. She would be there, I felt it in my gut. Before I could rethink my impulsive decision, I rushed out of the door.

I told myself that I just wanted to talk to her; that I just needed her to know how I felt. In her presence, somehow, the words wouldn't come. Surprisingly the tears...the tears came. Because being back in her space, I realized that I had made the biggest mistake of my life. I loved this woman. I stepped back into her world and became whole again. I could feel the rejuvenation within minutes of being in her presence.

I'm not an emotional person, yet the tears came. The anger that initially greeted me, dissipated as she witnessed my display of emotions. I didn't have to say a word. *She knew.*

"Why are you here?"

Contempt. Tears.

"Why are you here?"

Desperation. Confusion.

"Why...are...you...here?"

Resignation. Hurt.

She barraged me with questions for which I had no answer. Standing in front of her I still wasn't sure. I wanted her in my life, I knew that...but I still couldn't offer her what she wanted or needed from me. Hell I wasn't even sure she wanted anything from me anymore. There was someone else....someone willing, stable...better. So Keenan, I asked myself...why are you here? I was the same man offering her the same thing the last time we were together.

Nothing.

Yet...everything.

"I don't know."

"You can't do this Keenan...you don't get to do this. Why? Why would you come back here? I'm happy now...let me *be* happy."

I closed the gap between us and held her as we cried together. The last time we had a moment like that, we ended up making passionate love in her office. The night I went to her was different. There was too much between us. Still, it didn't stop my body from reacting to the nearness of hers. I stroked her hair, kissed her face. My own tears mingled with the flow of hers. I restrained myself from further contact. She didn't need a lover, she just needed...me.

Finally cried out, her awareness returned as she forcefully pushed me away. Her eyes were blazing when she turned to face me.

"What do you want from me?"

I didn't know how to feel about her pain. On one hand, it hurt me to see her hurting. However, that pain...let me know that she still cared. That realization gave me hope.

"I want you."

"No you don't. *You* walked away. You don't get to come back and interrupt my life."

She was right; however, I knew that I wouldn't have peace until I knew exactly how she felt. What I planned or could do with that information was beyond my scope of reason. For my own selfish reasons, I just needed to know.

"Do you love him?" Maybe that's what I really wanted to know: if she really loved Kyle...if she had indeed moved on.

"I don't owe you an answer to that. I am happy and that's all you need to know."

I couldn't accept that. Answers...that's what I wanted from her. I couldn't leave with doubts.

"Do you love him Toni?" She turned away and walked to her booth. Without prompting, I walked to the carafe of coffee and made a cup. I sat on the opposite end of the booth, facing her. Silence engulfed us as we sipped...the overcast skies, a dismal representation of our mood.

Suddenly she spoke without looking in my direction. "I love who he is to me...for me."

I closed my eyes as an instant sense of relief washed over me.

"Do you...do you still love me?"

She refused to take the bait. "I won't answer that."

Silence again....then tears, again. "I gave you...everything Keenan. You let me give you everything knowing there was no future for us."

That was something I would always regret. How could I change this? How could I make this better?

I stayed, for as long as she allowed me to. There were moments of conversation, moments of tears... moments of silence. At some point, I took a chance and reached for her hand. She didn't pull back. I finally left with nothing resolved. I at least left knowing that we were ok and most importantly, I sensed that she still loved me.

That...for now, would be enough.

Chapter 12: Inner Circle

Finally! The crew is meeting at Intermezzo for the first time in what seems like forever. I have been craving time with my girls. So much so, that I'm actually on time.

Keenan being back in Atlanta has my mind in chaos and my emotions all over the place. It had taken a year, but I had finally tucked him away in the recesses of my mind and heart. Now he's here. Not just a forgotten image from my past, but a walking, talking, breathing, very real version of himself. He is back in my space and it has not been without consequences. I have remembered...his scent, the feel of his skin, the touch of his face. I have remembered...my body has remembered...and now it's longing for more.

Damn you Keenan.

I locate a parking space and hurriedly enter the restaurant. Dawn is easy to spot at our once regular table. Her glossy black hair hangs in a straight blunt cut past her shoulders. Her makeup, of course, is flawless, and the strapless pantsuit she wears accentuates her lean curves. Always the diva, she has on heels even though it's fairly early in the day.

"Morning Diva", I greet her.

"Morning hun," she responds, wrapping me up in a warm hug. "Are you really on time? You must be starving."

Her comment provokes the meanest side eye. "I'm not entertaining this foolishness this early in the morning." She only smiles, as I signal the waiter over for drinks.

"And where, may I ask is Ms. Rae? Surely she's not *late* is she?" I ask with exaggerated concern.

Dawn laughs. "She and Mia should be pulling up in a few minutes. Girl you know it's hard to keep up with Rae since me and Lexie moved out. I miss my girl."

During this odd year of reconciliation, Dawn and Lexie moved out of the home they shared with Rae and moved with Jamie to a house he was renting in Lawrenceville, northeast of Atlanta. For the first time, Rae was left as the lone tenant in the townhouse that even I had once called home. She didn't have long to enjoy her solitude though. As soon as Mia got word that a spare bedroom was available she immediately called Rae and made arrangements to become her new roommate. By then we had all adopted her as our little sister anyway. Rae didn't charge her much, leaving her in a much better financial situation than trying to maintain her own apartment. It's proven to be a win-win situation for them both.

Actually, it's been great for us all. Since moving in with Rae, Mia has become an honorary member of our inner circle. Her youthful, raw, and honest perspective has been greatly welcomed.

Just as the waitress returns with our drinks, Rae and Mia walk through the door. Mia is casual chic in an off the shoulder top, jeans, and boots...Rae is also dressed down in jeans and a light sweater.

Rae is shaking her head in disbelief as they approach. I smile, knowing without a doubt that it is because of me.

"Well, well, well...surely hell must be freezing over."

Jokes withstanding, we greet each other with air kisses and hugs. "Stop it. You and Dawn are not going to clown on me this morning or I promise I will return to my old habits."

To my surprise it is Mia who responds. "Pleease Toni. No one cares about your little threats...we all know that as soon as you leave, those old habits will be back on faster than your jacket."

"Et tu, Mia, et tu?"

"Wow", Dawn exclaims. "The young one is officially acclimated." They all share a laugh at my expense.

We settle in with idle chatter until we order our food. Already it feels so good being surrounded by their companionship, love and laughter.

"You know," I state, "We have got to do better. I've missed y'all man. I mean, I see Mia every other day but I feel like I'm always stealing time with you two. Come on catch me up on the gossip. I'm so ready."

"For real Toni?" Dawn stares me down. "There is absolutely nothing going on at this table that's even remotely as juicy as what's going on in your life right now. I did not drive all the way here and pay for a babysitter just to talk about my boring, domesticated life. So spill it!"

I cross my arms defensively across my chest. I knew they wouldn't let me off that easy...they never do. Still, I don't want to talk about Keenan or Kyle. The situation is just too stressful.

"Really?" I pout. "I don't want to go first. I hate my life right now."

"Hate?" Mia reacts strongly to my choice of words. "Girl I'm so jealous of you. I mean it's hard out here for most of us single women but you have the attention and affections of two very fine ass men. Honey, pass one over here if you don't want them. I'll take either one please and thank you."

"Crazy girl," Rae chimes in, "You do remember that one of them is married right."

Mia appears unfazed by Rae's warning. "Yeah and in my current situation, I really don't care. I'll take the nights, the Mrs. can have the mornings."

"Mia!" Rae is shocked as me and Dawn collapse into laughter. "I can't believe you said that. You would really date a married man?"

Mia's eyes slowly travel around the table. "What y'all ain't gone do is judge me. I am so far beyond caring and consideration. Besides, more married men are approaching me than single ones and frankly, I'm tired of saying no. I need something...different in my life."

"So wait a minute," I ask, trying to make sense of this foolishness. "Does this mean that Mia Scott has finally given up on her lost poets?"

"For now my sister," she winks and smiles. "Only for now."

"Well then," I finish off my mimosa. "Somewhere beyond earth hell really is freezing."

"Well you better keep your little happy, skinny ass away from mine. I know that." Dawn warns.

"Oh Dawn hush," Mia easily retaliates. "Jamie is so not my type. He's a little...soft for my taste." I scoot my chair closer to Rae, not trying to catch any of the impending blowback.

"What?! What do you mean soft? My husband's not soft."

"Dawn really?" Mia does not back down. "If Jamie's hair was any longer he would be prettier than you. The truth is the light my sister. Embrace it."

"I'm not embracing that mess. Calling my husband soft. I'm from the D...I don't do soft dudes."

Mia throws her hands up in exasperation, "There it is...she stay reppin the D. Well apparently you need to start reppin the A my sister with that soft dude." Her joke prompts another round of laughter.

"Ok, ok, I didn't realize an amateur comedy act came with brunch this morning. Y'all going to get off my back. I don't have time for this when there's real dirt to be uncovered at the table." To my dismay, she turns her full attention back to me. "Stop stalling Toni and tell us what's up. Is Keenan really here in Atlanta...to stay? Have you talked to him? I tell you what...his wife is a dang fool. How does Kyle feel?"

I pause for a minute to gather myself after the barrage of questions. Everyone around the table is now strictly focused on me. Regretfully, I sense there's no way around this interrogation.

"Yes, yes." I concede. "Keenan is back in Atlanta, unfortunately to stay...well at least for now. And yes I have seen him."

Rae shakes her head. "Girl how I wish I would have gotten to that grand opening on time. I would have so loved to see the first time that you two saw each other. The one time I'm late and I miss the fireworks."

"*Their* faces?" Mia states. "I would have paid good money to see the look on his wife's face."

"I can't believe you guys are joking about this." I once again fold my arms across my chest. "It was horrible. You have no idea how damn awkward it was being there with Kyle, seeing Keenan...seeing Keenan with...her."

"You're right Toni." Rae quickly apologizes, reaching over to squeeze my hand. "I can't imagine what that ordeal was like. So how did you feel? How did he react?"

There is a brief moment of silence before I finally admit the truth to my best friends, "Honestly, the moment I laid eyes on him...every single buried emotion bubbled to the surface. Oh my God I forgot how beautiful he is."

"So let me guess" Dawn teases "You're still in love with him...poor, poor Kyle."

"I don't know...no...maybe? Yes, I do know. I am in love with him. I don't want to be but I am." There, the forbidden words are now in the atmosphere.

"So what are you gonna do about Kyle?" asks Mia, almost too eagerly. "Are you gonna leave him?"

"No!" That I'm able to answer with no hesitation. "That's a thought I haven't entertained. Why should I? Keenan may have unleashed his emotions, but as usual, it comes with empty promises. He can't offer me any more than he could the last time we were together. And I didn't ask...there's no reason to. I mean at the end of the day Keenan made his choice and it wasn't me. So I'm not going to sacrifice my happiness for someone who....hell he doesn't know what he wants."

"What do you mean?" Rae eyes me suspiciously. "Toni have you seen him since the opening? Unbelievable… have...you...seen him?"

"Why are you looking at me like that? It wasn't my fault. *He* came to see *me*."

Mia's head whips in my direction. "Just scandalous."

Dawn doesn't help the situation. "Ha! I knew today was going to be a juicy one. What happened honey? Dish the dirt."

Giving in, I go into great detail about Keenan's unexpected visit to Muse...his declarations...his tears.

"Oh my God," Mia's response is purposefully exaggerated. "That is so insane. I'm so loving being in the midst of the inner circle. Who knew it was this amazing?"

"Whatever Mia. This is not a joke. This is my life. My life that this...this man insists on disrupting." I lean down, putting my face in my hands. "God, sometimes I wish I could go back to that moment when I first laid eyes on him. I would slam the door in his face instead of inviting him in."

Rae gives me the side-eye. "No, you wouldn't."

"No I wouldn't." I admit. Again we all laugh. "Nope," I continue. "There's no way I would have ever left his fine, chocolate ass on those steps."

As the laughter dies down, Rae looks at me intently. "Seriously Toni, what does he want...and even more importantly, what do you want? At some point there has to be some kind of resolution. This cycle is unhealthy for the both of you."

Dawn and Mia both nod their heads in agreement. She hasn't come to any conclusions that I haven't already drawn. The thing is, I had a resolution...one that I was completely intent on following through with. Keenan Jackson forced me to come up with an alternative plan, and now he was changing the rules. Worse, I am allowing him to do it. Admittedly, I didn't have to open the door when he came to Muse. There was no rule that said that I had to allow his existence in my world. Yet, I couldn't seem to stop myself. He has a way of making me stretch beyond my own carefully constructed boundaries.

Thankfully, the conversation drifts to other topics of interest as we order, dine, and drink. Mia entertains us with her dramatic love life...Rae vents about her job, Dawn gives us details about her once again domesticated life, including the adventures of a growing Lexie. It feels like old times and I am glad that at least this part of my life is consistent.

Now if I can just get my love life under some semblance of control.

Chapter 13: Proof

This has not been a good week. Professionally speaking it has been fine. Things are moving along quite well. In fact, we have interviews lined up for the entire day in our search for a full-time associate. The plan is to steadily grow then be fully staffed with at least three associates by next year. Today will be the first step into putting that plan in action.

There have been many long days and nights at the office. I'm in a constant state of guilt for leaving Keenan to his own devices, but it is what it is. I have to do this...spend this time, this energy...make these sacrifices...in order to end up right where I have always been fighting to be. I just hope that when the journey comes to an end, Keenan and I are still standing.

This has not been a good week, though, so I am beginning to have my doubts.

I can't put my finger on it. Somehow we have become strangers coexisting in a common place. Keenan has been distant. By the time I get home, he is usually locked away in the finished basement, engulfed in his 'work'. By night's end I'm on my laptop in the home office we have orchestrated out of a third bedroom while he is lost in his own world of creative forces. We kiss on our way out of the door...we have small talk on the rare occasions when our schedules collide. Sometimes...I silently slip down the stairs and ease the door open to watch him. Even with the emotional distance between us, I can't deny how desirable he is in his own element. There are usually paint smears across his hands, arms, face...yet, there is something strangely seductive in the way he caresses the brush...the intensity he displays as he creates pieces of himself, the way he longingly, possessively gazes at the canvas. It has dawned on me that without words, his art is his best form of communication. So often he is silent, brooding...unwilling to share his emotions. Now I realize how often he speaks through his chosen medium. Silly me...I haven't been listening. Maybe that is why it was so easy for him to fall for someone else...someone who spoke the same language. I get that now. But now, something is missing, and unfortunately I don't have the time to figure out what that something is.

My instincts tell me that it has everything to do with Toni. I am not a foolish woman. I saw the way he watched her on our opening night. He felt *something*. Something that was lost but had been revived at the sight of her. I saw it in his face...in his eyes. Nevertheless, he promised that he was good and I can only take his word on that. I can only trust in him that no matter what, he will not seek her out...that he will remain...true. Still, he is distant and that concerns me.

I decide to take a break in between interviews. We ordered in lunch, knowing that it was going to be a marathon type day. Still, I only had time to grab a sandwich here, chips there. In my current mood, there's only one thing I need to cheer me up... my daughter's voice.

I am just about to give up on reaching her when Keenan's dad breathlessly answers the home phone. I swear he is the last man on earth to exist without the use of a cellphone. I have no doubt that Zy'riah is the cause of his lack of oxygen. She definitely keeps her grandparents on their toes.

"Hey Mr. Jackson, how are you? I'm calling to check on my baby girl."

"Oh hi Sarai. How are you daughter? It's good to hear your voice."

"It's good to hear yours too, although it seems like you've lost it somewhat," I easily joke.

"Yes. You already know what, or should I say who, is the cause of that. This little girl has me outside playing with this ball. She keeps me young at heart, but she wreaks havoc on this old body." We both laugh in our comfortable way. One of my greatest blessings has been having them as in-laws. They have always been so supportive, and are so great with Zy'riah.

"Where is my little tornado?" As I wait for her to come to the phone, Marcus walks past the door pointing towards the conference room. I take a deep breath. No rest for the weary.

"Hi Mommy."

Tears instantly sting my eyes as her tiny voice echoes through the phone. This...is another great sacrifice. Not having her near...not being able to see her, smell her...share her days. I miss her energy. Especially in times like this.

"Hey baby. How are you? Are you having fun with grandpa?"

In her child-like way, she gives me a long recount of her day's events. I feel so guilty, but I can only hope that she, as well as Keenan will come to understand and appreciate what I am trying to accomplish for me...for our family. As soon as things settle down I must get her down here. My heart is breaking with the distance.

Our conversation ends with me promising to kiss daddy. Before entering the conference room, I stop at the restroom to collect myself. The last thing I need is for Marcus, not to mention the potential employee, to see me in shambles.

As I walk into the room, I notice that our next candidate is already present and seated. I apologize profusely for the delay. Marcus' face is a predictable mask of irritation. This is one time that I don't care. I've worked my ass off all week so I deserve the few minutes that I took to spend with my daughter. Before I can even settle in he already starts.

"Sarai, I want you to meet Rayna Williams. She wasn't on the schedule to be interviewed today, but I reached out to her to come in for a face to face. We met at the grand opening."

Leave it to Marcus to spring this on me. I glare at him before plastering on my best corporate smile and turning towards the pretty, petite woman. She looks vaguely familiar. Perhaps I had caught a glimpse of her at the event. It's difficult to remember with so many faces and bodies that were paraded in front of me.

"Nice to meet you...Rayna. Well thank you for accommodating our last minute request."

"Please, call me Rae. And honestly Marcus, thank you for the open invitation. I appreciate this opportunity.

Rae? Then it dawns on me. I think back to the grand opening. Keenan had mentioned a Rae to Toni. She is someone who is also in the marketing/public relations field. Surely this isn't the same person.

"Rae...I believe we may have mutual acquaintances."

Her jaw tightens...her eyes narrow. The pleasantness that was apparent one minute before has now disappeared.

"We do." She answers without further explanation. She continues to stare at me without speaking...almost daring me to challenge her presence.

Marcus is looking back and forth between the two of us, desperately trying to figure out why the sudden chill has appeared in the room.

I chuckle. "Well should we get started then?"

With the awkward tension hanging in the air as dense as fog, I almost expect her to fail miserably. Instead, she remains poised, confident, and focused. As the interview progresses, I'm more than impressed by her level of intelligence and passion. Honestly, in a perfect world she would make the ideal candidate to add to our team. But this world, especially mine, is far from perfection. The only reason I am even entertaining this charade is for Marcus' sake. There is no way in hell I am going to hire anyone who even has the vaguest connection to Keenan's ex-side chick.

After the interview concludes, she soon departs, leaving Marcus with a hug and a kiss on the cheek. No pretenses on our part. We don't even bother shaking hands.

As soon as she exits the building, Marcus faces me. "What the hell was all that about?"

Wearily I slouch into the nearest chair. "Can we not talk about this? I'm tired Marcus."

He stands in front of me...his body, taut with tension. "Guess what Sarai? I'm tired too. I'm trying to build my business, expand my brand, so you know what that means? I barely eat, I rarely sleep...this," he dramatically sweeps his hands around the room. "This is my life. So if there's something going on in *your* life that impacts *my* business, you need to let me know. So again I ask you...what the hell is going on?"

He is angry...and Marcus can be a very intimidating force when he is angry. I watch him warily before stating my plea. "We can't hire Rae ok? She's friends with the woman who was having an affair with Keenan, so obviously I'm not giving her a job."

The laugh he emits is void of amusement. He pulls up a chair next to me, resting his elbows on his knees. The echo of his laughter fades, leaving us in an uncomfortable silence.

"You know Sarai, I vividly remember the first moment I met you. Even then I knew that you were a force to be reckoned with. You were at every company event...you were always in the faces of the right people...the hunger was there, undeniably. I knew to keep you on my radar. I knew that beautiful, young, hungry you would one day help me build an empire."

He leans towards me, reaching out to brush my hair away from my face. "This..."he glances around the room. "... this is my gift to *that* woman...the one I faithfully believe still exists. Still, I have to admit...sometimes I get worried. I worry that you can become blinded by the 'stuff' going on in your personal life. And I can't afford that."

In anger I snatch away from his touch. "You *doubt* me Marcus? How can you possibly doubt me? I've sacrificed time with my family for this company. I've moved thousands of miles from my home, left my daughter in another state...for God's sake, I've almost sacrificed my *marriage*, Marcus...for *your* company...*your* legacy. And you sit here and say that you doubt me. That's a slap in the face."

"I'm sorry to hurt you Sarai. Business aside, you know I have mad love for you...but business is business."

The internal pain is immeasurable. I can't believe he has the audacity to say some of the things he is saying to me. Marcus and I have been a dream team from the beginning. In some ways we have become the power couple that I always believed me and Keenan would eventually become. I never imagined this...this shattered fantasy of my life. I am right on the cusp of having it all...yet at the same time it still remains so elusive.

"How can I ease your doubts Marcus? By hiring this woman? I have given too much for that to even be a factor. What could that even prove?"

"Do me a favor." He answers, "Take the personal aspects out of it and look at this in a totally unbiased way. Rayna's had the best interview of the candidates so far. She has years of experience working in marketing and public relations. Another thing I can add is that I got the chance to talk to her at length...and you know what...what I saw in you then...I see that same potential in her now."

I can tell from the tone of his voice that he is resigned to having her join our team. I relinquish all power at that realization.

"So how am I supposed to trust her as part of my team?"

He stands up, kisses my forehead and starts walking out of the door without looking back. "Figure that shit out."

*****

The cool air circulating in the lobby is a welcome reprieve from the intense sun. Fall is allegedly upon us; however, there are still some days when it feels more like early summer. I've learned the weather in the south can be very temperamental.

I'm patiently waiting in the lobby of Metro Art Gallery, a small, upscale gallery in Vinings, owned by Atlanta socialite Besa Diaz. We became acquainted on the night of The Paul Agency's grand opening and soon after, she expressed interest in seeing some of my pieces. Thankfully, I still maintained my storage and was able to have a few pieces delivered for her viewing.

If our partnership works out, it could prove to be a huge opportunity for me. Even in the short span of time I've been in contact with Besa, my artistic spirit has been revived. I have to admit that it feels good being back in this city. My initial stay here wasn't long...still in some ways it seems like home.

The lobby of the gallery is an inviting, plush space. Although I haven't known her long, I can detect Besa's influence on the decor. The brilliantly lit room is decorated in colors that are vibrant...bold...full of life.

A pretty assistant at the front desk has beckoned for Besa after I provided her my name. In no time, she strolls into the room looking as gorgeous as when I first met her. Her long dark hair shifts in waves and hangs to the middle of her back. Her full lips are painted a sultry red. The dress she wears is a bold print that only someone with her curvaceous frame can pull off.

"Keenan...how wonderful to see you," she warmly greets me...her rich accent coating her words like honey.

"Besa." I lean in, gracing her cheek with a brief kiss. "You're looking as lovely as ever."

"Mr. Jackson," she purrs. "I cannot even begin to compete with you sir." I don't take her fun and flirtatious behavior too seriously. I've learned that it's just a part of her bold persona.

"Come, come." She beckons. "I've been looking over your pieces and I must say that I am thrilled about the chance to work with you. I am in love with what I see so far." With that she saunters off, leaving me to obediently follow her steps. She leads me down a long, narrow hallway which opens up into a large spacious office in the back. Here too her imprint is evident; everything from the choice of artwork to the vivacious colors and prints. At least it is tastefully done and not overwhelming to the senses.

Taking note of the room, I observe my art pieces carefully lined against the wall opposite of her desk. They are tagged in green, all except one that is noticeably tagged in red. One that I had actually forgotten was in my stash.

As if compelled by some unseen force, I am automatically pulled in that direction. For a moment I hesitate before tracing the edges of the canvas with my fingertips. I close my eyes, imagining that the soft earth-toned colors actually reignite the feeling of her skin.

In stealth-like fashion, Besa moves from her desk to my side.

"Ah....this one..." her voice trails off as her hands make their way next to mine on the canvas. "This one I have decided to keep for myself...there is such a passion...a longing in this one." Her penetrating eyes watch me closely.

"This one...is a beautiful work of art from a man obviously in love. Were you in love Mr. Jackson?"

Yes I was. There is no way to express that to her though. She knows that I am a married man. In fact, she has met Sarai face to face. This painting...this likeness is nothing remotely close to Sarai's real-life image. It is instead, one of Toni. This work, as I recall, was feverishly completed after an amazing night we shared together. For hours I had watched her sleep. When dawn finally broke, the first rays of light played magnificently across her mocha colored skin, the parts that were exposed through the tangled sheets. I had to capture it...that moment. In that moment, my heart ached with uninhibited love. Even now...seeing it with fresh eyes, the emotions are so evident, so raw. Yes indeed Besa, this creation was from a man in love...who is still in love.

I close my eyes again. All I want is to escape from this torment. When I open them Besa is still here, still watching me for some kind of reaction.

"You can't buy this one Besa." It is a command and a plea at the same time.

"No? What do you mean? *You* sent it here."

Exhausted from this emotional tug of war, I run my hands across my face. "No, I forgot it was in the storage. I never meant to send it. I can't...it can't be sold."

"Keenan," she folds her arms across her ample chest...slightly tilts her head to the side. "I am a direct person, yes? So I will be very direct with you now. I am far from naive. I've had conversations and interactions with your wife...so I know that this person, this woman is someone "incidental" yes? But see, that is what I love most about it. The mysterious element of this beautiful woman...one who stirs such a passion....a love so intense that you were compelled to capture the aftermath. That...Mr. Jackson...is very exciting...very seductive."

She steps closer...the faint trace of her perfume entices my nostrils. She traces her manicured fingers down the length of my arm. "You are a very intense man, Keenan. I knew it from the first moment we met. It resonates within you. You have the energy of a true artist. If you allow it...we can develop a very beautiful and *profitable* partnership."

Her words ring with truth. There is no doubt that entering into this arrangement would be beneficial to my bank account. I have done my research...Besa is more than talk. Still...

I stare back at the painting of Toni...the tangled sheets, the wild hair.

Exposed.

None of my choices over the past year have come without a cost. How high would this price tag really be?

Sigh. "Let's talk numbers."

A huge smile illuminates her gorgeous face.

"Let's."

Heard a song by Maxwell today
Old school joint on the radio
Took me back to yesterday
To an old school love I used to know
...Back to you

Whenever, Wherever, Whatever
Hearing the lyrics to our song
Makes me reminisce on our moments of pleasure
Bonded by a love once strong
...Can't forget you

Darius and Nina ...us together
Body language expressions of poetry
Soul mates...life vests in bad weather
In the end though you didn't choose me
...Still, I want you

Thought those wounds had finally healed
Realized the stitches have all torn apart
Hidden secrets long concealed
Are now exposed fragments of my heart
...I hate you

Still...I wish you peace in this life
My first love...you defined love
Through all of the pain and sacrifice
My heart still carries your song love
...I still love you

Chapter 14: Changes

This has not been a good week. Professionally, yes. Muse is blazing with business and we are steadily building our database of partnerships. Personally...well that's on a whole other level. Personally I can't seem to get a grip on one solid thing. For the past month, things between me and Kyle have been ok, but just that, ok. Even though I haven't seen Keenan again, his presence looms over us like a dark shadow. I knew the night he left Muse that things with me had changed. Undoubtedly, Kyle sensed it too. I'm not focused, my emotions are out of whack, and worse, my heart still aches for an unobtainable love.

Tonight though, there will be no place to hide. It's the night of Keenan's show at Metro Art Gallery. For obvious reasons, I don't want to attend. The last thing I want to do is spend a night in his presence. Feel the raw pain of having him so close...yet so far away.

But of course I will go to support him. If for no other reason than for all of the late nights I had spent with him while he worked...while he talked about the possibilities of moments just like tonight. I want him to know that I remember and I am not beyond celebrating his achievements, even if from a safe, emotional distance.

In fact, we have all decided that we will show up to support. Kyle is on his way to pick me up and Rae, Mia, Dawn and Jamie are meeting us at the gallery. After all, at one point in time, he was one of us...and at the end of the day, he and Kyle are still family.

At least I know if shit falls apart, my girls will be nearby. Especially Rae, who in her own way has been getting a very up close and personal dose of Sarai.

The wheels of life are forever turning. How ironic is it that my best friend would end up working for my lover's...well ex-lover's wife? *Crazy*. Initially, she had reservations about taking the job offer, but I strongly encouraged her to take it. I know she felt stifled at her old firm, and besides she seems to really like the owner, Marcus, who was more than willing to double her salary. Scoring a D.C salary in a Georgia economy is a great achievement. She would have been a fool not to take it.

All day I have been struggling with my choice of what to wear. Metro Art Gallery is a very small boutique style gallery, but from what I've gathered, it has very upscale patrons. I don't know the owner, Besa Diaz, on a personal basis, but I've seen several photos of her in Atlanta mainstream editorials. Her bio is impressive to say the least.

After great length, I settle on fitted black pants-you can never go wrong with black- heels, and a mid-sleeve indigo, top that purposefully emphasized the swell of my small, yet full breasts . Feeling rebellious, I decide to wear my hair in an untamed fro. I check the mirror and I am pleased with the reflection of a pint-sized Pam Grier staring back at me. Just as I complete the finishing touches on my makeup, the doorbell rings twice, then I hear the key in the lock...Kyle's way of announcing his arrival.

His footsteps echo down the hallway as he makes his way toward my bedroom. "Toni, where are you girl. I hope you're ready."

I gloss my lips one last time and hurry out of the bathroom just as he enters. We smile at each other as we take in each other's appearance. He looks incredibly handsome in fitted jeans and a rose colored button-down shirt. Not a color that any man would, or could wear, but it perfectly complements his golden skin tone. For Kyle, this attire is super casual, but the addition of his Movado watch is a strategic hint of just how "business" he is. I close the gap between us and kiss him fully on the lips. In spite of my increasing doubts, I am proud to call him mine.

When we break away, he eyes me intensely. He continues to stare as he traces my neckline with his long, slender finger. My body quivers slightly beneath his seductive touch.

"You are so beautiful love. Do you know how tempted I am right now to completely undo all of this work you've done?"

My smile grows in capacity. "Well thank you baby. You know we don't actually have to go, we can always...send some flowers or something." The suggestion is so ridiculous; it causes us both to laugh out loud.

"Ah Toni, how I wish it was that simple. Regardless of how strange things are between us right now, Keenan is still my boy...still my family. It's my turn to support him as he has done with me through life."

The tone of his voice is unnerving. I turn his face towards mine...again kiss him softly on the lips.

"That's why I love you man."

He chuckles. "It better be for more than that woman."

I try to push him away, but he pulls me in and rains kisses down the length of my neck. It feels good. Oh so good. We should be leaving but I allow myself the pleasure of his touch. His wet, hot mouth blazes a trail to my own. A moan escapes in measured breaths as he nibbles lightly on my bottom lip. Unable to resist, I reach down to massage him through the dense material of his jeans. There's an instant response to my touch. I break away from his heady kiss to lay my head at the base of his neck. My Kyle, my lover, my friend. I have always loved his smell. One that has always been familiar and a source of comfort. Now it one that seduces me…lures me in. Before we lose ourselves completely, he abruptly stops and grabs my hand.

"Come on let's get out of here before I really change my mind."

I want to stay in this moment; however, the spell is irrevocably broken. The clutches of reality rapidly sets in.

Keenan awaits.

****

The first thing I notice when we arrive is that the gallery is packed to capacity. If the myth of Besa's clientele is proven to be true, tonight should be a considerably successful one for Keenan. Although our lives have taken different turns, I still care deeply for him. It makes my heart happy to witness the manifestation of his dreams.

Kyle and I walk in hand in hand. The crew, Rae, Dawn, Jamie and Mia, are already assembled and huddled together in a tight space in the corner. Rae spots us and promptly waves us over.

"Good evening beautiful ladies and gentleman." I greet them as we file in, completing the circle.

"Girl you are looking HOT." That's quite a compliment coming from the Diva. "You know, you should think about dyeing your hair red. It would look fabulous against your skin tone."

Self-consciously I tug at my unruly coils. "What are you saying Dawn...that my hair is boring?" She rolls her eyes as everyone else laughs. "No silly...you are far from boring...I'm just saying some color would add some spice."

Kyle tugs the hair at the nape of my neck sending an instant shiver down the center of my spine. "Nah, she's spicy enough. I already have to fight to keep her." We all laugh again...although the underlying tone of his words is not lost.

Without missing a beat Dawn responds. "All I'm saying is, you wouldn't be fighting if you had stepped up to claim her, my brother."

"Really Dawn," Kyle dramatically grabs his chest and staggers back in an exaggerated fashion. "Really?"

Adding salt to the fictitious wound, Rae raises her glass in a toast to Dawn, "Truth!"

My icy glare encompasses the circle. "You know I'm glad petty Patties get so much humor at my expense."

Mia chimes in. "Come on Toni...admit it girl...it's funny right? You know it's funny."

"No it's not." I try to maintain my sense of indignation, but I lose the battle when I feel Kyle's lean, muscular form embrace me from behind.

"Ok," he teases, "Stop laughing. Y'all know artists are sensitive." For the second time tonight, I find myself pushing him away. "You know what..."

We continue to joke, laugh, and gossip for some time. Jamie and Kyle eventually leave to get drinks at the open bar leaving us girls to our own devices. As soon as Kyle is out of hearing range, Rae starts in.

"Alright girlfriend, speak on it. I'm dying to know what's going on in that head of yours."

Their eyes are watching me... waiting on my words to satisfy their hunger for drama. I shake my head. "I don't know what I feel Rae. I'm so conflicted. Inside I'm bursting with pride for Keenan, while at the same time it hurts like hell that I can't truly express it or...share it."

I gaze around the room filled with the appointed elite of the Atlanta social scene; all gathered to celebrate a man I once loved.

"So many nights...so many conversations we've shared about this very moment. He accomplished everything he said he would and we don't even get to share in it together." My throat tightens as I struggle to keep my emotions in check.

Mia sidles over to embrace me with a sympathetic hug. Before our conversation resumes we are interrupted by a sultry voice, just as exotic as the woman who bears it.

"Aye why such long faces. This is a celebration not a funeral."

Besa Diaz stands before us. She is a stunning woman, more so in person that in print. She has long dark hair that cascades in soft waves down her back, skin that is a glowing honey bronze, lips that are a tantalizing red, and a curvaceous body that is poured into a crimson pantsuit. I'm finding it difficult to take my eyes off of her, until... *he* steals my attention.

Keenan.

Once again standing before me... as gorgeous as Besa is stunning. His long dreads are secured in a bun at the nape of his neck. His goatee appears to be freshly trimmed...his cocoa skin gleams under the glaring studio lights. A form-fitting, black

V-neck sweater and jeans gloriously caress his sculpted boy. He is the epitome of the dark, reflective, beautiful, artist.

Lord help me.

We stare in brooding silence when our eyes find each other....each of us too afraid to speak in the company of others; fearful that our independent emotions will escape in the breaths of any conversation.

It is Besa's rolling tongue that eventually breaks the glaring silence.

"Keenan, these are your friends...yes? Are you going to make introductions or just stand there and continue to stare at this...beauty?"

Only then does he look away, obviously embarrassed by his temporary lapse of control.

"Yes, of course...good evening ladies...this is Besa, primary owner and curator of Metro Art Gallery. Besa, these are dear friends of mine...Dawn, Rae, Mia and...Toni."

We exchange greetings in unison. For one uncomfortable moment, Besa stares at me, then back at Keenan. He attempts to avoid all eye contact with her.

Rae speaks. "Besa you've done an amazing job putting this show together...and Keenan...oh my God, I knew you were talented, but not *this* talented! Your collection is amazing."

"Thank you so much Rae...really, thank you all so much for the support. I'm still pinching myself. It's hard to believe that all of this is really happening."

Dawn responds, "I can imagine. Your work speaks for itself though. In fact, I convinced Jamie's parents to come, and

I'm pretty sure that his mom has her eyes on at least two pieces."

"That's fantastic news!" Besa reacts. "You all had me worried for a moment...you were so somber when we approached." Although her words are aimed at the group, her piercing glance is only steered in my direction.

"No, no..." I hastily answer. "Just typical girl...stuff."

"Well," she responds. "Don't let me keep you from your....*stuff*. I just wanted to thank you all for coming out and for showing your support." She casually dismisses us, turning her full attention towards Keenan. "I'm going to speak to some of our other guests...find me in about thirty?"

"Yes...of course." He dutifully answers.

She gives a small wave as she turns to leave...the scent of her expensive perfume remaining long after she's disappeared into the crowd.

"Wow," Mia speaks in frank admiration. "That is *all* woman." Keenan chuckles as he watches Besa's retreating figure. "Yes she is definitely...something."

There is random small talk until Kyle and Jamie appear back in the circle with drinks in hand.

"Keenan."

"Kyle."

Their flat greeting is a far cry from their usual embrace. In time, I hope the wounds will heal. I can't bear the thought of being responsible for a permanent breakdown of their relationship.

Right on cue, Jamie whisks Dawn away to meet some "important" friends of his family. Rae and Mia soon abandon ship as well. I am left alone with the loves of my life.

"Hey man," Kyle begins, "I can't even begin to tell you how proud of you I am. I'll be the first to admit that when you talked to me about leaving your cushy job at the firm I thought you were insane. Now, it's good to see you following your heart."

"Thanks Kyle. That really means a lot." As he speaks, I can see some of the tension leaving his face and shoulders.

I use this moment of reprieve as an opportunity to escape. I don't know if I will truly ever feel comfortable enough in the presence of both of them...maybe in time, but not tonight. I touch Kyle on the arm, gaining his full attention.

"I'll leave you guys to talk while I check out some of the pieces. Keenan...congrats on everything." He nods in acknowledgement. Hurriedly, I make my exit, encountering Daniel and some of his business associates around the corner. We spend time conversing and networking before I finally get a chance to browse the collection and see the world through Keenan's vantage point.

The showing is comprised of a mixture of new and older pieces. It's good to see so many of his works with the infamous red stickers next to them indicating that they have been purchased. One particular piece catches my eye. It is one of two young boys perched on the stoop of a faded yellow house, which, from my recollection of past conversations, would be Keenan's childhood home. There's something nostalgic about the longing look on the young boys' faces. Candy wrappers surround their feet, as they laugh in an overstated, conspiratorial manner. My heart aches. I know the images depict a childhood memory of him and Kyle. In expert fashion, he has captured the essence of time...lost.

"This one is very interesting...yes?" I sense her presence even before she speaks.

Besa.

There is no denying the intoxicating scent of her perfume.

"Yes." I simply reply without facing her. "Interesting indeed."

Without further prompting she continues, "Keenan is what can be considered an old soul. His skills come not just from his hands, his mind...but his heart, you know. It's what makes his art very special."

I turn to face her then. She is watching me with her keen eyes, waiting...for what I'm not sure. I don't respond. In spite of her beauty there is something about her that is...unsettling. I see it then...the hint of calculation now exposed in her dark eyes. This is by no means a casual conversation. I search for any hints of truth but it all remains concealed.

"Yes," I agree, "Very special."

She smiles coyly before glancing around for nearby patrons. "Ah Toni," her tongue caresses my name, "do you know that he loves you?"

My head whips back in a state of shock. What does this woman know about me?

Instead of answering I simply stare back at her. She laughs. "That must surprise you yes? That I know of his heart...his...intentions."

"Listen Besa, I don't know what your aim is, but please don't fool yourself. You may not know as much as you think you do."

She laughs again, which is now beginning to grate on my nerves. The trace of her earlier charm is wearing thin.

"Do you find me that amusing?"

"No, quite the opposite bonita...I find you quite interesting. I want to know more about the woman who is my artist's muse."

Now it is my turn to laugh. "I think you have me mistaken for his *wife*."

She looks at me for a moment before smiling again in that irritatingly slick way. "Ok...well perhaps I am mistaken. If I offended you in any way, I apologize. Can we just start over bonita?" She extends a perfectly manicured hand. I hesitate before taking it. Who is this woman really? Why does she feel so comfortable making these kind of blunt allegations?

We settle into an uneasy truce.

She turns to leave, but I feel the need to warn her. "If I were you, I wouldn't be so reckless with my words. Whatever your reason for saying these things...it's disrespectful...to him and his wife."

She pauses and appears to contemplate her next words before speaking them out loud.

"Please, I didn't speak out of disrespect. Only truth. Perhaps one day you will both confront it, yes." Then as quickly as the words roll off her exotic tongue she disappears into the shadows of the room, leaving me feeling absolutely clueless. What truth does she speak of? What exactly does she know?

I refuse to waste my time giving it much thought. The encounter has left me with frazzled nerves so I abandon the painting altogether and forge a direct path to the open bar. Just as I receive my drink from the cute, flirtatious bartender, I'm stunned by the sensation of light fingertips on the small of my back. Butterfly teases send instant chills through my body. There is no denying who it is…only one person can make my body respond in such a way.

Keenan.

*****

Something happened. I'm not sure exactly what...but something happened.

At some point in the night I ventured off to find Besa, just as she requested. Turning a corner, I saw *her* standing at the bar. I stopped short, surprised to find her alone. Instinctively, I searched the room for Kyle...soon locating him on the opposite side of the room. As usual, he was talking to a group of distinguished looking gentlemen. History had taught me that he would be occupied for a minute. Kyle, always in the hunt for potential clients, has never wasted an opportunity to connect and network. Sarai had just stepped outside to take a call so, against my better judgment; I impulsively headed in her direction.

She was smiling at the bartender, as he handed her a glass of wine. For a brief moment I felt the faint stirrings of jealousy...possessiveness. Once, there was a time when I was the only man who could put that kind of smile on her face. Crazy but I wanted a minute to be familiar with her again. Without thinking, I touched the small of her back. A small gasp in response confirmed that in some ways, at least, I could still affect her.

The bartender scurried off, perhaps assuming that I was her lover returning to stake my claim. She slowly turned around to face me as I took a few steps back, not wanting to completely invade her space.

There was no indication that she was surprised to see me...proof that time had not made her unfamiliar with my touch. Her small hand clinched the glass, as she stole furtive glances around the room. Undoubtedly she was searching to see if Kyle or Sarai were within striking distance. I half expected her to take off in the opposite direction, but was pleasantly surprised when she actually stepped closer. Taking advantage of the opportunity, I closed the gap between us.

"Hey you." Our once familiar greeting habitually rolled off of my tongue.

"Hey." She blessed my presence with her beautiful smile.

"Well, glad we got that out of the way." I joked. "I wasn't sure if I should be prepared to fight or what."

"No Keenan." She easily laughed with me. "I don't want to fight with you." I was thankful for that. I just wanted to be Keenan...not her enemy...just the guy that used to make her smile.

"Toni, I know I probably shouldn't even be speaking to you right now...but I want to first off apologize for bombarding you the way I did the other night...that wasn't fair to you...and I'm sorry for that... It's just...when I saw you...*everything* came back. I think I just lost it for a minute."

She took a sip of her drink. "I know Keenan. Seeing you threw me for a loop too. It was...crazy...seeing you after so much time. I just...don't want there to be this awkwardness between us whenever we see each other. We're going to have to find a way to co-exist."

I responded to her challenge. "Trust, I won't make that any harder than it has to be."

She looked away and nodded silently before taking another long sip. For a minute I was mesmerized by the residue of wine that stained her luscious lips.

"I'm sorry Toni. I can say it a thousand times and it probably still won't make a difference but I am."

"Ok." She answered, watching me with those beautifully rich brown eyes.

Silence.

I pushed my luck and stepped closer. There was no sign of retreat.

"Would I be out of order if I tell you how beautiful you are tonight?"

There are boundaries I shouldn't cross, but when it comes to her I just can't seem to help myself.

She smiled. "I'll accept that."

Old stirrings awakened from slumber. I wanted to touch her. I even reached out halfway before letting my hand drop back to my side, suddenly remembering my rightful place.

I moved in closer. Again she remained planted firmly in place.

"Would it be disrespectful of me to say that...I miss you?"

Her breath became...still. Her eyes closed. When she opened them she looked right at me...through me, without speaking.

I wanted more. I wanted to savor the moment with her. Hold onto the conversation, no matter how tense or awkward. But, Kyle had ceased his conversation and from across the room, we made eye contact. There were questions in his eyes as he glanced at her and back to me. I gave him an abrupt nod, hopefully a fair enough indication that everything was all good.

It would be best if I moved on.

"So... I think my time is up love." I smiled in an attempt to ease the tension that we both felt from Kyle's blazing glare. Regretfully, I stepped back...putting necessary distance between us. "I certainly don't want to cause you any trouble."

She tilted her head to the side. A seductive smile played on her succulent lips.

"Mr. Jackson...you've been nothing but trouble since the first night I met you." The tone of her voice enticed me. I wanted desperately to prolong my time in her space, but she walked off in Kyle's direction, leaving me staring longingly after her.

*****

Reflecting back on that moment, I realize that something was different. Her response, her smile...it was different from the night at Muse. Then, she was angry, hurt, disappointed. Not last night. Last night she almost seemed...receptive. Of course it could all be in my head. Just foolish me... grasping for any sign that she still harbors any kind of feelings.

I have to get my head straight. Sarai and I are meeting at her office for lunch and the last thing I need is to be in my wife's presence with a mind overrun with thoughts of another woman.

I find the building with ease and make my way to the fifth floor. This is my first time being back in the space since the grand opening. Surrounded by windows and void of bodies, the openness of the room is more prominent. It is tastefully furnished with modern designs in muted shades of gray and navy. Understated...classic...powerful...an obvious likeness of Marcus Paul.

The office manager, Tammi (if I remembered her name correctly) is at the front desk. Her roaming eyes take me in from head to toe as I make my way to her station. Pretty bold considering that Sarai is her boss. If she doesn't know now, she will learn.

"Mr. Jackson," she warmly greets me, standing with an outstretched hand.

"Tammi." I respond with slight hesitation. Her satisfied smile lets me know that I've guessed correctly.

"Mrs. Jackson is in a meeting with Mr. Paul but she'll be finished shortly. Follow me and I'll lead you to her office."

"No need." I stop her. "I'll get there." She is clearly disappointed.

As I stroll down the narrow hallway, I pass the conference room where Sarai and Marcus are engaged in an intense conversation. Reports are scattered across the long table. In colorful script, notes, forecasts, and numbers are displayed on the white board behind them. This is her world...her element. This is the life that I have chosen to leave behind.

Sensing my presence, they both look up as I stroll past. I nod and keep moving, not want to interrupt whatever brainstorming session is taking place. I reach the end of the hall and enter Sarai's office on the left. Soul food is in carry out plates on a small table by the window. It's not until I'm confronted by the enticing aromas do I realize just how hungry I am. Hopefully Sarai won't be in her meeting much longer.

I walk over to the large window and stare out at the skyline of the city. Growing up in D.C., I never knew much about Atlanta, other than what was depicted in movies or through the music scene. Hip-hop groups like Outkast and Goodie M.O.B were instrumental in the city earning its nickname of the Dirty South. Gritty, soulful; standing here now, I can easily detect those elements. Yet, there's a side of Atlanta that many people don't talk about. Beyond the country dialects and brash attitudes, lies a city rich in culture and historical significance. There's a pride and swagger the city conveys being the birthplace of civil rights icons like Martin Luther King J.R. and Hosea Williams and literary gems like Pearl Cleage and Kenny Leon. It's unquestionably layered and I realize that I've only begun to scratch the surface.

The echo of footsteps interrupts my train of thought. When I turn around, I'm expecting to see Sarai. Instead, I'm startled to see Rae stumbling in, her arms overloaded with files. Somehow I have forgotten that she now works for the agency. This city man...layers and layers.

"Keenan", she starts, once she realizes my presence.

"Hey Rae... how are you?"

She meticulously stacks the files on the corner of Sarai's desk and comes around to give me a hug.

"I'm good...busy," she laughs, glancing back at the files. There is an uncomfortable moment of silence. All of our previous, social interactions have been through our connections with Toni and Kyle. This is different...a different time...different circumstances.

"What about you Keenan? How've you been?"

She and I both know that is a loaded question. Before answering I stare back out at the city. She follows my lead and quietly stands beside me.

"I'm not sure Rae."

For some reason a lie won't manifest. I am not "good" by any means. My emotions are all over the place and my mind is a jumbled mess.

She leans against the clear pane and turns to face me.

"Yeah I get it." She pauses again before continuing. "Can I be honest with you?"

She looks towards the door and starts again before I even have the chance to answer.

"You have to let her go Keenan. You love her...I get that, and I have no doubt that everything you feel for her is real. All of this...this is bigger than you...than the both of you."

Rae has never been a bull-shitter. I like and respect that about her. Even now...her bluntly stating her opinion... is right in line with her character. It has nothing to do with me but everything to do with who she is...a pit-bull, fiercely protecting her own. I can't be mad at her for that.

"I know Rae." My mood is somber. "I'm trying my best."

A long deep breath escapes her lips. We are both lost in our thoughts.

This being her city, her home, I wonder how different our perspectives are. Does she see the underlying beauty? Or does she only see the rawness, the "dirty"? Sometimes when you're right in the middle of something, it's hard to have an unbiased point of view.

Without engaging eye contact she simply questions "Are you really Keenan?"

Before any further conversation can be had, Sarai walks into the office, stopping abruptly when she sees us huddled together. Instinctively Rae steps back. We look at each other in silent acknowledgement that for now this conversation will be shelved.

Without another word she walks past Sarai and out of the door.

Sarai closes the door behind her, takes off her shoes, and seats herself at the table. I immediately join her and begin the routine tasks of unwrapping and plating food.

After several minutes, she speaks. "So, what was that about?"

I glance at her trying to gauge her mood. Her blank face gives me nothing.

"That" I respond, "was nothing but a conversation."

"Hmmm...ok." she states without sounding too convinced. I don't want to delve further into this conversation. Rae's words are ringing in my ears...especially since I recognize their truth.

I have not fully released Toni to just...be. I am the one who has been pushing up on her, showing up at Muse, seeking her out at the gallery. Somehow, I have to find a way to do better...be better. She has moved on and this isn't fair to Sarai. Let her be Keenan, I chastise myself. No good can come from this.

Yet, even as I attempt to commit the words to heart, I already doubt if I will ever be able to completely let her go.

Chapter 15: Complexity

Late again.

At this exact moment, I am supposed to be at Atlantic Station, meeting Kyle and Rae to watch the new Kevin Hart movie and grab a late dinner. We haven't been out together in a long time so I am looking forward to the evening. I feel in part to blame for the near disbandment of the Three Musketeers. Just a couple of years ago we were hanging out, clowning, enjoying time together. Then my "relationship" with Keenan happened and that ultimately changed the course of...everything. Who could fathom that one life decision could have such a domino effect on subsequent events? Knowing what I know now, I've wondered if I would I make the same choices as I did then. Would I choose to have him in my life? Funny...the more I've thought about it, the more I've realized that yeah, I would. In spite of everything I wouldn't change...anything. Blindly I've conceded that being loved by him was an experience worth the hurt, pain, and brokenness.

In fact, loving him, being loved by him, has changed my entire life. Changed my perspective...changed who I am as a woman. Before him, there were dates, sex, work...then more work, less dates, less sex. Muse was life...and life became Muse. Then he came along and loved me...and everything I thought I knew was redefined. It wasn't just the sex, which was from our first encounter, phenomenal. It was him "getting me", learning me, knowing me...in a way that no one else had. It's what made our chemistry so very real.

It's also the reason that I've decided to let go of the anger and attempt to co-exist with him in peace.

I can't pinpoint when it happened. This altered state of feelings. Maybe just being back in his same space has thawed the coldness that was conceived in his absence. I just know that when I felt his hand across my back, I didn't want to fight with him anymore.

When I turned to face him, I no longer saw the man who broke me. I saw the man I once loved. A man who once made me happy, made me smile...who "got" the best and worst of me, the man I once called my friend...claimed as my lover. Beautiful him...complicated in nature, complex in structure. He was back in my world and I...we...would learn how to make this work.

Maybe.

*****

Rae and Kyle are huddled together near the entrance of the theater. They both shoot daggers as I approach.

Kyle is quick to chastise. "Seriously Toni... I told you to leave Muse over an hour ago. What happened?"

"*Seriously* Kyle, we're only missing a hundred previews."

"Guess what?" He retaliates, dragging me towards the attendant poised to take our tickets, "I actually *like* previews."

*****

Three hours later and we find ourselves in Copeland's Bistro: eating, drinking, and recapping highlights of the movie.

With perfect timing, and grand luck, we were able to get a table. The restaurant is unusually crowded for a Sunday night. There must have been an event in the adjacent courtyard.

The conversation has somehow steered towards Kevin Hart's life and career.

"That brother has always been about business," notes Kyle, signaling the waitress over to get a second round of drinks. "You have to respect his hustle."

Rae is not impressed. "His hustle, I respect, there's no denying that...but you know what I hate. I hate that just like so many other brothers out there, he reached the pinnacle of his career, and what did he do? He left his wife! The mother of his kids...the woman who stood by him when he was just broke ass, lil ass Kevin."

I laugh, "Rae, you don't know anything about that man's business. You have no idea of what he and his wife were going through before he became famous. Maybe there was just a disconnect that became more prominent after the fame, the women, the tours, the movies. Who really knows?"

I could have saved my breath because she doesn't buy any of it.

"Whatever...trifling...that's what that is. I heard she got very little in the divorce settlement too. Two kids and she gets nothing? Trifling."

"Ouch." Kyle reacts as if she has personally attacked him. "Rae, we have been best friends forever, and I am still absolutely baffled as to how you've become so cynical. Your dad and brothers are some of the best men I know. Where did all...this...come from girl?"

I've often wondered the same thing. When I first moved to Atlanta, and subsequently met Rae, her family welcomed me with open arms. I was a naive country girl trying to find her way in the city. Her brothers, in a sense, became my brothers and they protected me just as fiercely as they protected their own. Maybe that's why Rae is so strong-willed. She's always been blessed to maneuver in a world with an intimidating force behind her.

She smiles conceding the truth. "I know right. They are, but that's why I won't take bull-shit from any of these clowns out here. They have to meet my daddy's standards."

"Girl," I shake my head. "Since you obviously can't marry your daddy, you better come down off of that high horse before you're riding into the sunset by your damn self."

They both laugh.

"Go ahead and laugh. I promise you that would fine with me...nope...wouldn't bother me one bit."

The conversation lingers as the next round of drinks arrives. Just as we are about to do our customary toast, we see a familiar face coming towards us.

Marcus Paul.

There's a noticeable change in Rae's facial expression. Very rarely do I get to see her with that "look." Hmmm...perhaps little Ms. Rae isn't as immune as she claims she is.

"Marcus." She casually greets him when he arrives at the table.

"Ladies...Kyle. Sorry for this intrusion, but will you guys mind if I crash your party? The wait is over an hour long even for one person."

Rae searches our faces trying to read our thoughts on the interruption.

It is Kyle who answers for all of us, "No man of course not. We barely got in ourselves before the rush."

Without hesitation, Marcus seats himself in the vacant chair next to Rae. The slight tension in her body is the only telltale sign of her reaction to his presence. It is easy to see why.

Marcus Paul is indeed a handsome man. Tall...even taller than Kyle...smooth brown skin and an athletic build. He certainly carries a powerful and commanding presence.

I suddenly realize that I don't know much about him. He and I have only met him once, at the agency opening, but Rae speaks highly of him and that alone carries much weight.

We make small talk and order desserts-the restaurant is known for their variety of cheesecakes-while Marcus orders a drink.

"You're hanging out by yourself?" Rae questions. I can't tell if it is out of general curiosity or if she is just trying to gain further insight into his private life.

He smiles before answering. "Yes...I've been so caught up with getting the agency off of the ground that I haven't been able to devote much time to my personal life. So, I just decided to get out of the office today... get some fresh air...explore the city."

"Shame on you Rae," Kyle teases. "You mean to tell me that you haven't offered to help your new boss get acclimated to our wonderful city?" A light flush colors her cheeks. If looks could kill, he would be six feet under already.

Marcus laughs, reaching over to touch her lightly on the arm. "No, it's fine. I would never impose on Rae like that. She has to put up with me Monday through Friday so I won't force her to deal with me on her private time. I can be...intense...to put it mildly." His dark eyes never waver from hers.

"Yeah Marcus," I chime in. "Rae is a pure bred Atlanta born peach. You *have* to take advantage of that."

She stares me down and kicks my leg under the table.

"She's that good huh? Well then maybe I need to reconsider." He leans closer to her, by now, picking up on the overt vibes we are throwing their way. Her body instantly stiffens at his nearness; nevertheless, he doesn't budge, taking great pleasure in her state of discomfort.

"Oh please," she tries to calm the escalating tension. "Kyle and Toni are clearly exaggerating. Marcus, anytime you want to hang out or tour the city...just let me know. Besides, you're not that difficult to handle."

"Well that settles it," he agrees, extending his hand. She hesitates briefly, before making contact.

For a few more hours we enjoy our grown folk night out. As the night progresses, Marcus and Rae seem to get more comfortable with each other. I've concluded that I really like Marcus. Not only is he gorgeous, but his intelligence and ambition are evident. I'm glad Rae decided to make the move to join his agency. I have no doubt that under his wings, she will find the success that unjustly eluded her at the other firm.

I excuse myself to find the restroom and Rae instantly follows suit. As soon as the door closes I pounce.

"So...you want to tell me what's going on with you and Mr. Marcus?"

"Don't you start with that foolishness Toni." She quickly dismisses me, refreshing her make-up in the oversized mirror. "There is absolutely nothing going on between us. Marcus is my boss *only*...you know I don't get down like that."

"Yeah that sounds good friend...but you're not going to insist that I'm only imagining the chemistry between y'all. I swear if it gets any hotter, this bistro is going up in flames."

She can't help laughing. "Look, I'm not denying how...*delicious*...he is. I'm just saying that I try and keep my life as stress and drama free as possible. You know that. Besides the last thing I need is to have my name attached to more ridiculous rumors of me sleeping with my boss. I am not trying to go through that mess again."

"Mess" is an understatement. Rae went through hell at her old firm. One of her co-workers started vicious rumors of her sleeping her way up the corporate ladder. Regardless of how she fought against them, the rumors just wouldn't die. She tried ignoring them but in the end there was collateral damage. Promotions stopped coming her way as well as offers for her to be on special projects. Her immediate supervisor tried to protect her, tried to fight for her, which only made matters worse. Getting the unexpected opportunity at Marcus' agency was a life-saver...much less a career saver. There's no way she would risk the chance of messing that up.

"I get it girl. I really do. Damn shame though. Well, he seems more than a little infatuated with you so keep your guard up."

"Don't worry. I'll keep him close...just not too close." She smirks.

Abruptly she turns my way as if hit by a sudden thought. "Speaking of keeping your guard up...I saw Mr. Jackson today." She searches my face for a reaction to his name, although I'm not sure what she is expecting.

"Ok...at the office?" She's not giving me much to work with as I try to determine where this is going. A nod of confirmation is her only answer. I can't say that I never expected this to happen. Keenan is now her boss' husband so I knew she would have more interactions with him; however, if she thinks that I want a play by play of his comings and goings then she is dead wrong. The less interest I have in Keenan Jackson, the better. While I no longer consider him an enemy, we aren't exactly best friends either. A peaceful existence is my only goal.

"We talked about you...sort of."

That piece of information does peak my interest. Why would I be their topic of conversation? My name should be taboo anywhere remotely near Sarai's presence.

"Ok Rae what is this? Why are you being so freaking cryptic? And why are you and Keenan discussing me, especially at your place of employment? That's not exactly wise on his part or yours for that matter. Didn't we just establish that you're not trying to get fired?"

She rolls her eyes in exasperation. "Of course not Toni. It just...happened. Anyway...the details don't matter. What matters is the fact that that man is still in love with you."

I turn my attention towards the mirror... run my fingers through my untamed hair. Without looking her way I state, "So he says Rae. We both know that doesn't mean anything. He has the life he chose...and I have the life I've...reconstructed. What else is there to discuss?"

"What else? Let me tell you something girlfriend. Here's what was absolutely confirmed for me yesterday. That man has not let you go. And he's *here*...not in D.C...he's here in Atlanta on a permanent basis...and that, is trouble waiting to happen, Toni. I can't let you keep walking around with your head in the sand."

I can't contain my frustration. "Rae, I don't have my head in the sand. I'm well aware of how Keenan feels. Still, I can't let his feelings impact my life. I don't want to think about it every day. I have way too much going on...Kyle, Muse...he's not on my list of priorities."

"Ok," she answers without much conviction. "Well I just hope you remember that when he comes for you...because I have no doubt in my mind that the day will come when he does exactly that. And there are too many innocent bystanders who can easily get caught in the crossfire."

The discussion for now is over. We return to the table where the men in our lives await. Kyle looks up and smiles. I smile back but my mind is light years away as Rae's dire warning echoes in my ear.

He will come for you.

Chapter 16: Forbidden

It is an "all hands on deck" kind of day at Muse. We have been incredibly busy, which is typical during exams at the local colleges. The crew, including Mia, who thankfully graced us with her presence after her last test, has barely eaten or rested.

The phone rings and I instantly recognize Daniel's office number. I answer and put him on hold, as I rush to the office to pick up on that extension.

"Make it quick Daniel, we are swamped today."

"That's always good news," he answers and I can only imagine the smile on his face. "Listen I just wanted to brief you on a conversation I had today with Besa from Metro Art Gallery...you remember Besa don't you?" He pauses, waiting for me to give some sign that I did remember.

How could I forget? Her words still rang suspicious truths in my ear.

"Yes," I answer.

"Good, well we talked about doing a fundraiser/art gala at Muse, which I think will make sense for both businesses. She can gain access to our clientele and we can pool from hers...a win-win situation. Can you or Tanya stop by there today to hash out the logistics?"

"Besa? Really Daniel?" The last thing I want is to have any kind of dealings with Besa Diaz. Her unknown motives make me uncomfortable.

"Yes, really Toni." There is frustration in his voice. "Besa has a powerful influence in Atlanta. Besides, if we're serious about expanding, we're going to need the extra exposure."

"I understand that...it's just..." My voice trails off, not really knowing how to vocalize my thought. This is just one of those times where I need to put aside my personal bias for business. Internally, I know the advantages of connecting with Besa, but she is connected to Keenan and I don't need that kind of proximity right now. It's apparent that he is already too close for comfort.

"Just what Toni? You know that I'm right on this. I thought you would be more excited. I don't understand where this hesitation stems from?"

Of course he wouldn't. Daniel Moore is my partner, not my friend. He doesn't know the complex history of me and Keenan.

Instead of answering, I divert the attention back on him. "If it's that important then why aren't *you* meeting with her?"

"I can't. I'm flying out to Charlotte tonight for a conference. I won't be back for at least a week."

Fantastic.

"Ok," I unwillingly relinquish my reservations. "I'll check in with Tanya. Either way one of us will meet with her and we'll connect with you when you get back."

"Great....I'll call her and let her know that one of you will be over this afternoon. I'll also text you her cell number. And Toni, should it be you, please fix that attitude."

*****

Just my luck Tanya isn't available to meet with Besa due to a pre-scheduled parent-teacher conference at her son's school. Meeting with Besa is the last thing I want to add to my to-do list. It's not that I don't like her. She just rubs me the wrong way. Especially with the comments she made about Keenan...me. She is definitely a slick one. One possible silver lining: maybe this could be an opportunity for me to dig deeper into all that. Or, on second thought, maybe I should just leave well enough alone.

After it slows, I hurry home in order to change into something more suitable. Having already been in Besa's presence I know to at least be presentable when we meet again; two professional women on equal grounds. After a brief scan of my closet, I pull together a light jacket with a vintage tee and choose a pair of slim fit black jeans and boots. Not exactly Fortune 500 but definitely artsy-chic, which in some ways is better suited for the Gallery. On my way out of the door I grab a band and gather my hair into a careless knot.

As usual, traffic is a mess but I still manage to arrive with minutes to spare. I rush in, only to be informed that Besa isn't anywhere on the premises. Beyond irritated, I get her number from Daniel's text and proceed to call her. I pray that I haven't wasted my time. She answers and I hear the frustration in her voice.

"Besa, hi, it's Toni. I'm at the gallery."

"Ah Toni...I'm so sorry bonita, my meeting ran late, and now I'm stuck in this horrible traffic. Are you able to wait? It may be another hour at least."

Who am I to chastise anyone for tardiness?

"Sure. I'll just grab some food or coffee then meet you back here. Take your time and be safe; I'm free for the rest of the afternoon."

"Thank you for your patience my dear. I'll call you when I'm closer... yes?"

"Yes," I accept. "That works."

I think about how to bide my time until our meeting. I'm grateful at least, that I don't have to drive anywhere. The Gallery is in a prime location...various restaurants, coffee shops, and trendy boutiques line the plaza. I'll just walk around until I see something that I want.

He walks in just as I am about to walk out.

My breath catches in my throat. What is he doing here?

He stops short when he sees me, looking around as if he's waiting on someone, anyone, to step forward and declare that he's being punked.

"Toni." There is a measure of disbelief in his words.

"Hey...Keenan." My words are casual, while my heart is racing. I wonder if a time will ever come when my body doesn't automatically respond to his presence. There's just something about him that draws me in; a certain connection...chemistry... that exists beyond our level of comprehension.

He is casual in jeans, sneakers, and a light hoodie. His dreads are also pulled into a loose knot at his neck. There is slight twist of irony in that. Once, there was a time when we would have enjoyed freeing each other's manes from their unwanted constraints.

Stop it Toni, I mentally scold myself. Funny, I have only been in his presence for five minutes and my thoughts are already making a mean left turn.

The awkwardness of the moment covers us in a blanket of silence until he actually speaks.

"What...what are you doing here? Where's Besa?"

I explain Besa's absence and give him a run-down of our meeting.

"I'm going to take a wild guess that you're here to meet with her as well."

He sighs...rubs his hands across his beautiful face in that way in which I'm familiar. I watch his movements, my heart aching with that knowledge. It used to be so good, knowing him in that way.

"Yeah, I am. She lured me in saying she has a new opportunity for me and I'm guessing this...event with Muse is what she has in mind." He suddenly laughs, his rich voice echoing through the gallery. "Ah Besa, you little slick woman you."

Clarity finally dawns on me. "Wait a minute. Are you one of the artists she's showcasing for the fundraiser? I guess I should have known. I don't know why I didn't grasp that."

Still in disbelief, I sit on the stylish bench by the front entrance. How is this supposed to happen? For some reason, I am absolutely sure that we can't be in each other's presence for an extended time without there being some repercussions.

Without prompting he sits down next to me. Even in my distressed state, I can feel the heat radiating from his thigh.

"You know what. Don't worry about it. I'll talk to Besa and fix this. She has other artists who can easily fill that slot."

"No Keenan, you don't have to do that. This will be great for your career. I mean...we can do this... right?" I need his reassurance. Need so badly for him to tell me that we will be ok. Instead, he stares at me with those soulful eyes...smiles that gorgeous, magnetic smile.

"Sure love." His words seduce me and I realize that we are indeed in *trouble.*

*****

Sometimes I can't figure out if the Gods are against me or strategically working in my favor.

As I headed to the gallery, my only thoughts were of the new opportunity Besa had for me. It was hard for me to contain my excitement. I have to admit, she is certainly making good on her promise to propel me to the next level. So good in fact, that I have been feverishly painting, trying to make sure that there's enough supply for the impending demand.

Typically, I don't like working under these circumstances, nevertheless, with my numerous life dilemmas; there's been an abundance of themes trapped in my head. It's actually been a blessing to be able to get it all out. Good or bad, I've tossed it all up and let it land as it may. Out of that chaos beauty has been created. It's crazy how that shit happens. I just need to narrow down the pieces I want to share.

Seeing *her* stopped me dead in my tracks.

There's just something about being in her presence. Her beauty...her essence...always seems to overwhelm me. I try so damn hard, but my heart always seems to find its way back to her.

Thinking back, we should have stayed within the confines of the gallery. Yet, once again, I couldn't resist testing boundaries. It was my suggestion to get some food while we waited on Besa's arrival. Truthfully, I expected her to decline my offer. That would have been the right thing to do. Then again, when have we ever been on the path of righteousness? Instead, she accepted...yes, there was a brief moment of uncertainty...still, in the end she accepted.

We walked, talked, laughed...enjoyed each other's presence as we once had the privilege to do. God I'd missed that sexy, husky laugh...those effortless conversations. We've always had the ability to talk about anything and everything....without judgment...without pretenses.

We were so engrossed in each other that before we realized it, we were back near the gallery. Still hungry, we entered a small café and ordered sandwiches, coffee and dessert. All the while, the conversation never ceased. She talked about Muse, the possibility of expansion; I talked about my upcoming projects. We tried to keep things on a superficial level, but there was no mistaking the unspoken chemistry that was brewing between us...always existed between us. I felt it, every time she looked at me. Saw it, beyond the mask of indifference I knew she wanted to portray. I wanted to savor every word from her tongue...taste their residue on her lips.

That is, until reality snaked its way in and I was harshly reminded that our present was just another stolen moment.

It was the sound ringing of her phone that disturbed our solitude. *Kyle.*

He wanted her to know that he was coming over...that he was bringing takeout. Ordinary, mundane acts committed by people who are in casual relationships. Their conversation ends with the customary *goodbyes* and *I love you's*...ordinary... mundane words...depending on your personal perspective.

She didn't face me after. In fact, neither of us said anything. The moment was briefly tainted by unspoken feelings...shame, hurt, pain. Forbidden feelings that shouldn't be explored nor explained.

Yet, we do exactly that.

"Sorry." She whispered with downcast eyes.

"You don't owe me an apology Toni."

"I know...still...I'm sorry." The weight of our unspoken emotions was a heavy burden to bear. I made the decision not to carry mine anymore.

"It's hard Toni...seeing you love him...accepting the fact that he gets to love you."

She turned to face me. Her eyes seemed to penetrate the heart of me.

"And what makes you think that this is easy for me Keenan? I have to see you with *her*. Living a life that I once thought was my future."

I closed my eyes...drew in a deep breath. "I know. I know...it doesn't keep me from missing you...miss loving you." I shouldn't have said those things, but we had already crossed prohibited lines.

She reacted with a slight laugh... the effect of my words evident in her raspy tone. Absently, she shook her head, as if that motion alone could keep the memories of those passionate nights at bay.

"Yeah we were good weren't we? I'll admit...I do miss that...sometimes...that certain energy we had."

"Cosmic." The only word to adequately describe it.

"Cosmic." Her whispered breath enticed me. "Yes."

As if the word itself invoked action, she cautiously reached for me. Instinctively I reached back...intertwined my fingers with hers. We sat in silence...relishing the opportunity to touch, to feel...to *remember*. I rubbed my thumb across her palm...noted the sharp intake of breath.

Familiar stirrings re-awakened.

I brought her hand to my lips...planted soft kisses on her fingers. She tried to mask her emotions, but the small whimpering that escaped her throat gave it all away. She was undeniably affected.

More...I wanted more. I had to have at least a taste of her. My urgings and growing desire overwhelmed my sensibilities.

Without releasing her hand, I went to her. I was grateful that her side of the booth was partially obscured from the view of the other patrons.

"Keenan." My name softly spoken from her luscious lips. It released the last remnants of restraint that I barely held. I sensed her reservation, but I didn't yield.

I kissed her...and the once forgotten taste of vanilla was delicious on my tongue. All I wanted was a little taste, but I should have known better. She has always left me wanting more. I sucked ravenously on her lips...invited her tongue to dance with mine. It wasn't long before we found our familiar rhythm.

She responded with unbridled passion and equal hunger. I expected her to hold back, but she gave me...everything. She sucked my lips as if she was thirsty for the taste of me.

Me. She wanted...me.

I claimed her.

Until, once again her phone became an unwelcome intrusion.

We departed, instantly snatched back into our existing reality.

"Yes." She answered breathlessly, her eyes never leaving mine. "No we're together...at the café across the street. We're coming right over."

"Besa." She confirmed.

"Toni," I started, reaching for her once again. The moment, though, had obviously passed. Physically she pulled away, but still reached out...her fingers lightly traced the length of my face.

"No Keenan."

The finality of her tone stung. What could I do? I didn't have the right to be selfish...she had already given me more than I deserved. We exited the booth...paying our tab at the register on the way out. As we reached the entrance of the gallery, I noticed that Besa was already there...waiting. She greeted us; her cunning eyes filled with suspicion as glanced from Toni to me.

I looked away, unable to face the unspoken accusations in her eyes.

How could I have answers for her, when I couldn't figure out the answers for myself?

Chapter 17: Sanctuary

"Let me get this straight. You are conducting business with Toni...*Toni?* Please dear husband. Enlighten me as to how that transpired."

I pour myself a glass of wine and walk back over to the sofa where a stack of documents and files await my undivided attention. My plan was to give them exactly that; that is before my wonderful husband, in the most nonchalant manner possible, announced at dinner that he will be doing business with his ex-mistress. I still can't imagine how that happened. As far as I knew, there had been little to no communication between them. I'll admit, when I saw him and Rae huddled together in my office, I was more than suspicious. I don't know her well enough to understand her motives. Other than that moment though, he hasn't given any indication that he's been in contact with her. In fact, even at his showing, he seemed to keep his distance.

So to say I'm blind-sided by this revelation is truly an understatement....and I'm more than curious as to how it's come to this.

He leaves the stool at the bar and comes to sit next to me on the floor. Dressed casually in a tank top and pjs, with his long dreads cloaking his shoulders...he exudes sexiness. Yet, there is weariness projected through his eyes. I can tell this is a discussion he'd rather not be having; however, if he expects for me to go along with this senseless plan, he has no choice but to start talking.

"Look, don't blame me," he pleas, "blame Besa. She and Daniel, one of Muse's partners and investors, came up with this fundraiser idea that would garner more publicity and exposure for Metro Art Gallery and Muse. Besa just told me that she had a great opportunity. I didn't even know until yesterday that it had anything to do with Muse...Toni."

I rub my eyes, feeling my own state of weariness settling in. I swear I'm so tired of hearing her name. This woman is given more attention in my household than she deserves. I take a sip of wine, completely over this situation. All I want is peace in my household.

"And once you found out, why didn't you decline? There will be other opportunities Keenan. You don't need this."

"Yes I do Sarai. I wouldn't even be discussing this with you if I didn't. The show was a great start, but we both know it was only the beginning. I need this exposure if I'm really going to build my name...my brand."

He leans forward on his knees, clasps my face in his palms.

Try as he might, I refuse to be deterred.

"So exactly what will this venture entail? How much time are you going to be spending with her? I made it very clear when we got here that I was not giving her an all access pass to my husband. I mean it Keenan. I don't want any bullshit from you."

"I don't know Sarai. Not much I presume. I have two new pieces to submit, but other than that most of the logistics will be worked out through Besa. I don't anticipate spending time with her other than the day of the event."

This doesn't feel right. Everything in me tells me that this is not right. I need more answers than what he is giving. I need more...truth.

"Keenan, have you seen her, talked to her?" His hands leave my face as I simultaneously reach for his. I search his deep brown eyes for some clue, some emotion... some semblance of truth. Keenan has never been a good liar. Asking him directly will get me the answers I want.

Instead of answering, he closes his eyes...shielding his truth from my sight.

"Yes."

Yes.

I'm in such a state of disbelief, that I'm literally speechless. Why didn't he tell me? What is he hiding?

My hands release their hold on his face. I tug on his free-flowing dreads. It is my way of commanding his attention. He opens his eyes; a veil of secrecy now firmly in place.

"When?"

The details of their alleged, incidental contact spew forth. His words spin a vague tale of them waiting...talking. He does not say that they spent time reflecting...reminiscing. He does not say it, but I know it happened. My instincts tell me it did.

"Why didn't you tell me?" I watch him closely for signs of deceit.

"Why would I? Being there wasn't about *her*. It was about *this*....business. That's all."

That's all.

History has taught me that when it comes to him and this woman...nothing just...*is*. And the way his eyes shift when he makes his declaration confirms my suspicions.

Oh Keenan. Either he is much weaker than I believed or she is a much stronger foe than I anticipated.

"You've never been a good liar Keenan."

"Sarai," he starts but I deliberately kiss him, sealing off the flow of his words. I allow myself the pleasure of feasting on his soft, full lips. He responds...tasting the sweet coolness of mine. It is good, but it is different. For a moment, I just want to end the conversation and just lose myself in the comfort and pleasure of his touch. But I can't give him this...not when he has secrets. I pull away.

He doesn't fight me. Instead he gets off of the floor and sits in the chair next to me...rubbing his hands across his face.

"Something...happened."

He doesn't deny or affirm...he just sits silently in the chair, staring blankly at the floor. The sting of tears catches me off guard and frustrates the hell out of me. Who are you?! I want to shout. I want so desperately for him to be the person I fell in love with but I'm beginning to realize that *this* man is, and may always be... different.

She changed him...made him complex...intense, when he used to be so...easy. I can't reach this man. Yes, I know how to keep him close, but I...I don't know how to penetrate this blank, void, exterior.

Truth be told, I'm getting tired of trying. It shouldn't be this hard to love someone. Not someone you've known and loved half of your life. I want to keep our family intact; but he has to want it...I can't drag him along on this journey. I refuse to do that.

"What do you want me to do?" He asks, still unmoving.

His audaciousness humors me.

"I'll leave that up to you husband. I'm not going to babysit a grown ass man so you do exactly what it is that you...want...to...do."

With that, I gather up my neglected documents and retreat alone to the faux sanctity of "our" bedroom...the distance between us widening with each step.

*****

The taste of him still lingered on my lips. A taste that in reality was better than my richest memories. I should have stopped him...that would have been the right thing to do. But having him so close...enjoying the familiar conversations, reminiscing on moments past...I found myself once again entranced by him. So when he came to me...offered me his taste...my yearning overpowered my senses and I couldn't resist.

I just wanted a little taste. Just to quench my thirst. Now... I have bitten the forbidden fruit, and I've found myself wanting more. Even in that brief, stolen moment, my senses had awakened with the feel of him, smell of him...that taste of him. In that moment I surrendered all inhibitions and remembered all that was good...and real...and raw.

Now I can't forget.

"Hello...earth to Toni, earth to Toni." The sound of Mia's voice breaks through my reflections.

"Girlfriend, what or should I say who, in the world has you this far gone? You have been walking around here like an extra on The Walking Dead."

I shake my head, as if that act alone can erase the memories of yesterday.

"I'm sorry Mia." I apologize, heading straight to counter where she has just placed a freshly brewed carafe of coffee. She follows me, relentless in her quest to obtain answers.

"No need to apologize my sister. Just give me some details please. What's really going on in your life?"

I laugh, eyeing her warily. "When did you get this nosy?"

She's quick with an answer. "I have always been nosy...I just never had the privilege of asking."

As we ease into my corner booth, her mood sobers.

"Seriously Toni, what's going on? Your mind seems a thousand miles away. I know you well enough to know when you are distressed."

Instead of answering, I turn my attention to the streets. The lunch crowds have dispersed so they are fairly empty. It is an overcast day, but thankfully there is no other sign of rain. Bleak and partially vacant...exactly how I'm feeling.

"I don't know Mia. I just have a lot going on."

"Does it have anything to do with Mr. Jackson?" She asks bluntly.

I turn to her. "Why would you say that?"

"For real? Come on Toni. I'm not delusional and you are not as slick as you think you are." She laughs. "Ever since he's been back you've been...different. Now, I may be young, but I'm old enough to know that the only thing that can make a woman come undone is a man. And not just any man mind you."

I simply stare back out into the gray nothingness. If Mia can so skillfully pick me apart, I don't know how I will manage concealing these...emotions...from Kyle's keen sense of perception. I've been trying really hard to keep it all together but I have to admit that the situation is slowly and methodically unraveling.

I rub my temples, weariness settling into every fiber of my being. I feel as if I've lived twenty years in one. This is one time in life where I could use a re-do button. So many things I would change, so much damage I would undo. Truthfully though, even if such a thing existed, I can't see never meeting Keenan. That old saying, "it's better to have love lost, than never to have loved at all", plays through the recesses of my mind. Even though I've lost him, I wouldn't change having been loved by him. As much as I love Kyle, Keenan was the best love of my life. Is...he still is.

"Mia," I finally respond, "I don't even know where to begin. I will tell you this little sister, the heart is a powerful weapon. Don't underestimate it."

She nods... for once, not having much else to say. My mood, I'm sure deters her from further inquiry. Usually I can laugh my way through, but she is right, I'm different.

She hugs me lightly, and returns to her post at the register. I remain in my own self-imposed solitude for as long as I can...until I realize that enough time has passed and it's time to get back to business.

*****

After some time, Mia knocks on the open door. "Uh Toni, sorry to interrupt you but there's a woman here to see you."

Other than Kyle or on certain occasions, Dawn and Rae, I rarely have visitors at the office.

"Who is it?" I mindlessly ask. For the past hour I have immersed myself in the latest reports, so I'm not into wasting time if necessary.

Instead of answering, she glances down the hall then steps into the office, obviously attempting to be discreet.

"See here's the thing. She didn't give me her name, but I'm pretty sure it's Keenan's wife."

I immediately look up and lean back in my chair. Surely she is mistaken. There is no way in hell that Sarai would dare infiltrate my sanctuary.

"Keenan's wife Mia? Are you sure? Do you even know his wife?"

"I think so," she answers skeptically. "I've never officially met her before, but I remember seeing *this* woman with Keenan at the gallery. I'm assuming she's his wife. Red hair?"

Sarai.

I close my eyes and try to keep the impulsive stirrings of anger at bay. What does she want? Why is she here?

"It's her right?"

I open my eyes to Mia's eager face. I nod in confirmation.

"What do you want me to do? Tell her you're busy?"

What do I want to do? Avoid this impending conversation at all costs. There's only one reason that Sarai would be here. *Keenan.* I haven't even come to terms with my own feelings and here she is seeking...I'm not sure what she's seeking, but it can't be anything good. Feelings of shame and guilt wash over me as I think of our stolen moment together, our...kiss. How can I sit across from this woman knowing what I shared with her husband?

"No. Just bring her back. Wait...on second thought, I'll just follow you out." She is already infiltrating my space. No need to give her any more power by bringing her in the heart of my business.

The front space of Muse is dominated by her presence. With an air of confidence she stands, casually observing the space around her. Her exotic red bob frames her beautiful face and she is dressed impeccably as usual in a fitted gray pantsuit. Self-consciously I reach to smooth my unruly coils.

Mia narrows her eyes at Sarai before one long glance back at me. I smile in her direction. She is around if I need her, although I don't anticipate the situation getting that out of hand.

"Sarai." Hard to believe there was a time when I couldn't say her name. It was easier then, to pretend she wasn't a real person, that she was just some lingering ghost of the past. Now, unfortunately, I'm accustomed to saying her name, accustomed to having her as an increasing part of my reality.

I hate it.

"Toni." Her response is emotionless...flat. There is a certain coldness in her eyes. Or maybe it is hate. Either way it makes me uncomfortable.

Without further words, I turn and walk to a booth in the back that is usually reserved for Mia's studies. She follows without prompting.

"Why are you here?"

There is no need for small talk or even the pretense of cordiality. We are not friends.

She laughs. "Well then, let's get to it." Underneath the laughter there is a glint of fire. "Let's talk about you and my husband."

I wait to see where the conversation is going. Does she know about our afternoon together? I'm not sure of her angle or the extent of her knowledge about me and Keenan.

After I don't respond, she continues.

"So...Keenan tells me that you two will be working together. Let me be very clear. I am not happy about it. I don't want him around you. I...don't...trust...you. But he's my husband and I know that this event is important to his...career."

She hesitates...waits. I give her nothing...just continue to watch her in silence.

"Look Toni, I don't know what's up with you two. I know there's more than he's letting on. Surely as a woman, you understand my instincts. I'm just here to tell you, if you're talking to him, stop. If you're seeing him...stop. If you're even texting him...stop. Don't come for what's mine, sweetheart. This is *my* husband, *my* family. I won't let you claw your way back in."

Now it is my turn to laugh. Who does she think she is coming into my space, making demands? I have no allegiance or loyalty to her. I owe her nothing.

"You really came all the way here to say that to me? Oh Sarai, here I gave you so much credit. First," I sit up in the booth. Out of my peripheral vision, I can see Mia looking in our direction, as if sensing the altered course of conversation. "I didn't come for your husband. He came for *me*...so if you want to make demands and set restrictions on someone, let that be *your husband*. Second, I don't have to claw my way back into anything *sweetheart*. Truth be told, I'm pretty sure I never left. Again, if you need clarification on that talk to *your husband*."

Although she tries to mask the hurt, for a brief moment it is exposed. The anger I felt just a minute ago is already dissipating. This isn't me. I am not the woman who engages in a heated argument in public with another woman over her husband. The absent feeling of shame creeps back in.

"Listen Sarai, I don't want to be here arguing with you in my place of business. This is not the time or the place. You've made your point. I just don't even understand why you're here. Keenan made his choice, he chose you. Why are you so concerned about me?"

Her steel glare shakes me. "I'm not a fool Toni. He came home. However, I'm not blind to his feelings for you. Keenan is only a man...a man who has weaknesses. He may falter, but he can't blatantly fail unless you open that door for him. He can only go as far as you allow him to. And woman to woman I'm telling you...warning you...don't open that door."

I couldn't let her get the last word. Not here.

"And in the spirit of honesty, let me just state...woman to woman...if you really wanted that door to remain closed, you should have been smart enough not to bring him...back."

She smiles warily before standing to leave. At the last minute, she turns as if to sling one last jab, but apparently decides against it. Without further retorts she walks out of Muse, just as graceful and elegant as she walked in.

The confrontation, so to speak, leaves me in a state of mixed emotions. Sarai is proving to be a complex woman. Are her unveiled threats really something I should even be concerned about or are they just additions to a long line of empty promises from another Jackson?

Again I find myself massaging my temples...trying desperately to assuage the headache that is simmering beneath the surface. Mia wastes no time hurrying over.

"Sis, are you good?" Her pretty face is marked with concern. I try to give her a reassuring smile. Feelings of guilt are now companions with my shame. I've always prided myself on being a worthy mentor and big sister. I never expected that she would have to see me embroiled in this kind of messy situation.

"Yeah." I respond, "I'm good."

In some ways that's truth. I am actually good. I have unwillingly faced the enemy and survived. Yet, there is an unsettling feeling in the pit of my stomach that I can't seem to shake.

Keenan Jackson may have been a storm to be reckoned with, but Sarai is gearing up to be a massive hurricane.

With sudden clarity I realize that I am not prepared for either.

Chapter 18: The Space Between

I grab the closest parking space to the front entrance of the gallery. I am ready to get this day over and done with; a day I find myself in high demand. Today is the official set-up at Muse for the fundraiser happening in two short days. All of the participating artists are meeting at Muse to handle the logistics of the space such as placement and hangings. Toni has enlisted my help, not unusual for an event of this scale. Keenan has also enlisted my services in getting some pieces transported to Muse from his storage and the Gallery.

Truthfully, I don't know how to feel about the event. Normally, I'm excited whenever anything happens regarding Muse. Why wouldn't I be? There's nothing more attractive than a powerful woman, and Toni is becoming just that with the growth and expansion of Muse. For years I've envisioned the life that we could have together, a life of prominence, security...happiness. Over the past year it seemed that dream could actually become a reality. At long last, my patience, support...blind love...was being rewarded.

Now though, everything is...different. The space between us is growing further with each passing day. She tries to mask it. Tries to act as if everything we had before is still intact. Still...it is different. It's difficult to pinpoint a cause; however, somewhere in the far creases of my mind, I sense it has to do with Keenan.

As far as I know they've had very little contact with each other. Of course, that's only what I know. If something has happened beyond that, I'm not aware of it. If there is anything else, that could only mean there is deceit and betrayal going on behind my back.

That kind of hurt would be...unforgivable.

So I don't entertain the thought.

I have to admit, though, I was surprised when she told me about the fundraiser. Not about the event itself. It's a great idea and an opportunity that I wouldn't expect Daniel to pass up. Still, I was surprised that she didn't put up more of a fight. I know that we've co-existed in an uncomfortable truce with Sarai and Keenan, but the last thing I expected was for her to tell me that they would be involved in a venture together. I didn't think we were that comfortable.

And it unnerved me to think that somehow they were.

For that reason, when Keenan put out the call for assistance, I gladly accepted. I need some time alone with my cousin...to see where his head is at; more importantly...to see where his heart is at.

*****

I see him as soon as I walk in. I hang back, as he seems to be engaged in an important conversation with Besa's assistant. The room is in a state of disarray. Various sized paintings are stacked against walls. From first glance the works are exceptional, at least from my limited, artistic perception. I'm thinking they should sell well at the fundraiser.

Noticing my presence, he signals for her to hold before strolling towards me with outstretched hands. No hug, as was our normal greeting for years. Yeah, things are definitely...different.

"Kyle, what's up man? I really appreciate you coming through for me."

"No problem at all. Toni has designated me as the errand boy for today anyway."

He laughs easily, however his face bears a slight trace of tension at the sound of her name.

"That's good. I didn't want to inconvenience you anymore than I have already."

That is an understatement. His presence alone is becoming more of an inconvenience than my life can handle. Nevertheless, I choose not to voice my opinion. At the end of the day he is still family and I will always be there for him when he needs me.

"So...I went by your storage unit and got the pieces you wanted. Tell me what we're taking from here so I can get it all loaded up."

For the next hour we work persistently to finalize his choices. On the drive to Muse, I anticipate having our discussion; however, he spends most of the time on the phone with Besa. By the time their conversation ends, I realize that we only have a few minutes to spare before we arrive. I guess we'll have to table our discussion for another day.

Muse is closed for the day with all of the activities happening. In fact, the only people roaming about are selected artists and the hired crew enlisted to assist with the manual labor. Already the space has been revamped. A few of the regular dining tables have been replaced by chic bar tables and stools. Artistic pieces are hanging meticulously and strategically around the room.

Mia greets us as soon as we enter.

"Well, well the beautiful ones are in the building."

Keenan laughs and gives her a hug before making his way toward the crew.

"Back off little one. We're both taken in case you conveniently forgot." I tease her.

"Please don't remind me Kyle. Besides, I know you have another cousin or something stashed away. Hook a sister up. The struggle is real my brother."

"What happened to Slang?" I ask with feigned concern, well aware of the running joke between her and Toni.

"Slang? For real Kyle you and Toni both play too much. His name is Slay... anyway he's out of the picture. Too moody."

I laugh, wondering if she'll ever find what she's looking for among her collection of lost souls.

"As much as I would like to play Iyanla and fix your life right now, I ain't able girl. You're too much. I'll have to start charging you consultation fees." She reacted by playfully punching me in the arm.

"See this is why I love-hate you man. Let me hurry up and get your woman for you before she ends up with damaged goods."

"Thank you." I call out after her as she flounces down the hallway leading to the office. Soon after, Toni appears. Any trace of my earlier concerns, disappear when I take in her appearance. Her casual attire of fitted joggers, and vintage tee, gloriously accentuates her ample curves. It amazes me how she is so petite, yet voluptuous at the same damn time. In typical fashion, her hair is in a mess of wild curls that perfectly frame her face.

My love...my dream.

Within minutes the eyes of every man in the room are on her...including Keenan's. All at once, I am hit by a barrage of conflicting emotions: love...jealousy... pride. Before she completely reaches me, I meet her half-way, engulfing her in my arms. She responds by wrapping her slender arms around my neck.
"Hey beautiful." I whisper softly in her ear.

"Hey you back."

I cherish this opportunity to hold her close...inhale her scent. In this moment we are ok and it feels as right as it always has in the past. Until...I feel her body tense and she pulls away ever so slightly. I know then that she has seen him.

Once again... *different.*

I loosen my grip. She steps back...separation complete.

Instinctively, I turn towards Keenan. Even though he has looked away and busied himself with the tasks at hand, I am aware of the tension in his jaw...the rigid set of his shoulders. Although our relationship is no longer on the level it once was, there's no detracting the fact that he is a man I know. A man I once called brother. Knowing him, I know that being in her presence has affected him. Without conversation, I have incidentally found the answer to some of my lingering questions.

My eyes find her again. There is an uncomfortable moment of silence that passes between us. I reach out to brush her thick mane with my fingers. She closes her eyes and I feel her own tension release in a long seductive breath.

"That feels good."

She, I once called my best friend. I know her too.

"Your man knows you girl."

Just like that, we are good again.

I grab her hand, leading the way to her favorite booth in the corner. We settle into our normal routine, catching up on the day. In great detail, she fills me in on everything that has been done and everything that's still on the to-do list. No worries, I assure her. I promise her that every task will be completed on schedule. She smiles and reaches for my hand. The evidence of trust is present in her eyes.

Always her constant.

Keenan comes over a few times, but only a few. Each instance, one in which he needs her specific direction. His avoidance is painfully obvious, although nothing that either of us cares to acknowledge or discuss.

My phone rings and with dismay I see that the number belongs to one of my colleagues. Reluctantly I answer and she informs me that we are having witness issues for one of our cases going to trial next week. As she provides me the details, I realize that the problem won't be resolved unless I actually go into the office. I end the call and face Toni, full of regret. I can tell by her own look that she already knows the outcome of the call.

"You have to go."

"Yes love." I confirm, standing to leave. "I am so sorry but I have to go in and figure out what's going on with this witness. With trials so close, I can't afford to let this case fall apart. I promise I'll be back as soon as I can."

She stands with me. "No worries. Handle your business. Your girl got this."

"I'm sure you do." I kiss her on the forehead. As I walk out of the door, my instincts direct me to turn around for one last glance. She is looking in my direction and gives me a small wave. In the background, there is Keenan. He doesn't notice me because he is too busy watching her.

Yeah it's definitely time for a conversation.

*****

After Kyle's abrupt departure, I have every intention of avoiding Keenan. Between our forbidden kiss and Sarai's unexpected visit at Muse, I realize that I am being pulled too far into another whirlwind of chaos and confusion. I don't want or need that in my life at this point. It was too hard the first time around...too painful. I am determined to get my emotions in check and let him go. But, as always, it's way too easy to get sucked back in.

I catch a glimpse of him and without thought, respond to his nearness...even as Kyle's loving arms encircle my waist. For whatever reason, I pull away. It isn't intentional. It's as if my body has an automatic response that is beyond its own means of control. I'm pretty sure Kyle felt it...that sporadic hesitation. There's absolutely no reason for me to feel guilty for loving him...especially in Keenan's presence. Yet...I did...and that...is indeed a problem.

Hours pass. We have navigated the morning without much interaction. Yet, even with the best of intentions, a time arrives when we unwittingly find ourselves alone...again. Inwardly, I curse fate. Mia leaves for class...the crew disappears for lunch. They have all served as my protective barrier against the man who once had my whole heart.

Hiding seems appropriate, as I settle into my booth with my own light lunch and coffee. It's not long though, before he casually slips in on the other side. His presence doesn't surprise me. He always seems to...come.

"What are you doing Keenan?" He answers with *that* smile and I can't resist smiling back.

"Why are we doing this?" He questions, reaching for some of my chips. "Why are we walking around on eggshells? It shouldn't have to be this hard...should it?"

"Don't play Keenan." I chastise. "You know why we have to do this...we do this because left to our own devices we steal secret kisses in the corner of cafes."

He leans back, absently rubbing his hands across his face. "Yeah I know. I'm sorry. I should have never initiated that. It's just so damn hard not wanting to love you when I'm around you."

I squirm under the heat of his gaze. His dark eyes travel to my lips, take in the swell of my breasts. There is no attempt to hide his growing desire. Once again he smiles...and once again I am disarmed.

"Stop...Keenan."

"Ok, look...let's go back to our truce. I won't come for you and you...don't respond to me."

"You better not come for me." I warn. "Your crazy wife is already showing up at Muse; the next time she may be crazy enough to show up at my house."

This news seems to catch him off guard.

"Wait, Sarai came here?"

"Oh yes...you didn't know? She practically threatened me...told me in specific terms to leave her husband alone."

"Damn...I didn't know that. I knew she suspected something happened the day we were...together. I tried to down play it, which apparently didn't work."

"Of course it didn't work Keenan. There will always be things that women just know. That's why this...has to stop. Nothing but trouble can come from this."

"I know Toni. I just...I know we're not together. I know I messed that up, but I don't want to lose you again. I know with one hundred percent certainty, that I can't live without you."

My heart breaks at the sound of his words. Words that I needed to hear a year ago, not now when I have moved on.

"I don't know what you want from me Keenan."

He stares out of the window before calmly turning to face me.

"I know that I don't want to be your friend Toni."

"Well then you should have chosen me."

Instantly his face is bathed in guilt. "I would give anything to change that. All you ever have to say is yes Toni...and I'll give it all up. If you ever decide to give me another chance, I'll be here waiting."

It's hard to bear witness to these raw emotions. Hearing his words fill a void I didn't even know existed in my soul. Still, my heart can't trust it. Crazy...this is a man I once trusted with everything. Then...he failed me. So his words alone hold little value.

"I can't leave myself vulnerable like that again Keenan. We were so good...our love was perfect. Then time happened and you proved to be...just a man."

174

The silence is suffocating. I don't want to fight with him anymore so I throw caution to the wind and go to him. His entire body reacts to my nearness but he doesn't face me. I lean against his back...bask in the warmth of his skin...re-acquaint myself with his once familiar scent.

It is not righteous to miss him as much as I do...but, I do. It is not right to allow myself this moment of guilty pleasure, but I do. In the midst of our silence, the music continues to play softly in the back ground. The smooth, rich voice of Donny Hathaway envelops us. The irony of that doesn't fail to escape me. On so many nights that very voice enticed us in pleasurable...passionate moments. I close my eyes and imagine for a minute that we are back in Keenan's small apartment. That our slick, naked bodies are tangled among a mass of blankets as we recite words of poetry and sooth our raw, parched throats with cool sips of fragrant wine. I imagine that he is mine, and I am his...and together, we are...*everything.*

Just for a moment.

It is not good for either of us to stay in this place. So I start talking. Not about us, just random conversation about life...Muse, the crew, even Lexie. The tension eases as he laughs and reluctantly responds. He understands my method. Without much effort we fall into an accustomed level of comfort.

We separate only when the first crew members begin their return. My heart heavy with the weight of my emotions, I slip out of the booth and start the mindless task of cleaning the table. He follows my cue and stands to leave. Before disappearing, he leans in close and whispers,

"Next time."

Chapter 19: Reality

Relentlessly, the sounding alarm interrupts my fading dream. For a moment, I am disoriented, unsure of when or even how I fell asleep. The display on my phone reads 6:00 p.m. *Damn.*

I must have hit the snooze button and knocked back out. I was supposed to be awake and up an hour ago...needing time to go into the office before attending tonight's fundraiser. This is why I hate mid-day naps. Too often, I end up feeling more exhausted than refreshed.

I sit up, steadying myself on the edge of the sofa. The house is fairly dark with the exception of a thin sliver of light streaming from underneath the closed bedroom door. Soft music drifts from that same direction. Standing, I follow the trail of breadcrumbs in search of my absent husband.

I expect to find him reading as he sometimes does. The sheets are obviously disturbed; however, the bed is empty. Above the music I hear the distinct sound of water running from a shower. I almost go to him...*almost.* Once upon a time, joining my husband for a shower would've been so routine, so common, so...easy. Now, our life, our relationship...has become anything but. There is distance between us and I'm not foolish enough to believe that it doesn't have something to do with...*her.*

I hate her. It's not a word used in my every day vocabulary. Still...I hate her. It's not just the fact that she slept with Keenan. No. It's the fact that I know he loved her, for the fact that his love for her almost destroyed my family, the fact that he can love someone so very different from who I am. It makes me question his love for me. Has he been settling all along if he could fall for her so easily?

I see it. Whenever I'm in her presence I see all of the things that he could love. She's beautiful...free-spirited, artistic. In those ways she is his perfect complement. At least for this Keenan...one I once was able to constrain...control. This Keenan found her and his inner spirit was unleashed. The problem is... I don't know how to reel him back in.

And that puts distance between us.

I wait for him on the bed. It's not long before he exits; toweling his long, thick dreads. His glistening body is beautiful in its bold, stark nakedness. Underneath his breath he sings along with the latest song on rotation. He stops when he looks up and discovers my presence in the room.

"Hey. Sorry, I didn't realize you were awake. The music didn't wake you did it? I turned it up loud enough for me to hear in shower."

He wraps the towel around his waist, conspicuously concealing his nakedness.

Yes things have certainly changed.

I beckon him towards me on the bed and he heeds my silent command. He grabs a pillow, lies in my lap, and stretches out his toned chocolate legs in front of him...something he hasn't done in a while. Back at Howard, we spent many nights like this, in this same position, talking about everything under the sun.

Funny...it used to be so easy then...to talk...to listen...to love. Where did it all go wrong? Why did he have to change?

"You didn't wake me. I needed to be up anyway to go into the office."

His hand finds the exposed skin of my thigh...traces light, loving patterns with his fingers. There is distance between us but it doesn't stop the awakening sensations between my legs. I massage his scalp through his damp hair. He's always loved that.

"The office? I thought you were going to Muse," he questions.

"Don't worry, I'll be there. There's just some paperwork Marcus wants to review with me, then we'll go over together."

In spite of my caress, a deep frown creases his forehead.

"Be there Sarai. It's important to me that you're there."

His vulnerability is endearing. *He needs me.* This is the Keenan I used to know.

"When have I ever let you down love?"

"Never." His brilliant smile lights up his face. The traces stop as he sits up and looks me directly in the eyes. Without warning he leans in to kiss me. The sweet taste of his tongue fills my mouth. Instinctively, I reach for his face to pull him in closer. His silky skin is still damp underneath my fingertips. My head spins with his intoxicating scent.

My eyes close as his luscious lips find their way to the folds of my neck, the swell of my breasts. He reaches my nipples and kisses them to erection through the thin fabric of my t-shirt. Kisses turn to small, stimulating bites. I almost lose it. I can't contain the moans that escape my throat. His own breath has become ragged with want. His beautiful mouth abandons my breasts and starts a slow agonizing trail down the length of my stomach. He continues downward and I grab the headboard in anticipation of his final destination. His hand grabs my thighs, forcefully spread them apart. He pauses for a brief moment and stares at me. My body trembles under the heat of his smoldering gaze These are the times I miss, long for. The times when we are good together. As good as we used to be when we were in the early years of loving each other. When our love was sufficient. When only we could quench each other's thirsts.

My eyes are closed when that first lick occurs. I cry out in shock and instantly grab his head to pull him in closer to my liquid heat. He grabs my ass and brings me closer to feasting lips.

"Yes Keenan! Oh my God baby." He doesn't bother removing my panties, he just expertly maneuvers around them. His tongue has thoroughly aroused my swollen clit. With each taste he has me on the verge of erupting. *I love how this man loves me.* My thighs are drenched, but he greedily laps my juices as if daring any to escape.

"Let go Sarai. Let go baby." His sexy, hoarse voice coaxes me to the brink. I can't hold on. My climax is forceful, as tiny quakes erupt throughout my entire body. He holds my pussy hostage until my journey is complete. I scream his name the entire time I ride the wave...until I am abandoned in an absolute, depleted state.

*****

Afterwards he comes to me and wraps his warm body around my still trembling frame. He plants soft kisses on the back of my neck. I close my eyes and try to hold back the tears that threaten to come. We have shared an incredible moment; however there's a sense of shame that lingers after the act. I should have denied him, but my body betrayed me. No doubt, my mother raised a strong woman, but Keenan Jackson has always been my greatest weakness.

Until he failed me.

Reluctantly I pull away.

This Keenan...this Keenan doesn't fight for me to stay.

Instead he draws in a deep breath, rolls off of the bed, and stands to gaze vacantly out of the bedroom window. His forgotten towel discarded on the bed, he makes a wondrous sight bathed in the partial light.

"What are we doing Sarai?"

Just like that the tone has shifted. He needed me...needed to love me just a few minutes ago. Now he's questioning our very existence. I won't keep doing this...dance. I can't.

"That's not for me to answer Keenan. I'm the same woman offering you...*everything*...like I always have for all of these years. *I've* never changed. So really the question is...what are *you* doing?"

I wait for an answer...something...any kind of emotion or reassurance. None is forthcoming. The silence in the room is deafening.

He finally answers but doesn't turn to face me. "I...I don't know how to love you anymore. I don't know how to fix this."

I almost answer. *Almost*. But I am exhausted. Too exhausted for this never ending tug-of-war.

Without responding I head to the shower. I have a sudden, urgent need to wash off the remains of us. What was beautiful only moments before now seems more like a solemn parting gift.

I want nothing more than to bail on tonight, but it's not who I am. No, I won't let my husband down. I will be in attendance and celebrate his accomplishments. I will rain down accolades and be his biggest cheerleader.

I will be the perfect wife...all the while pretending like in reality our shit isn't falling apart.

*****

An hour before the fundraiser begins, a charge of nervous energy surfaces on the scene. Last minute adjustments are being made, artists are huddled in their evasive conversations, and the media outlets are already arriving. In true Daniel and Besa form, there is an orchestrated "red carpet" style set-up in the front of Muse that is soon to be alive and active.

When I walk through the door, Toni is the first person I see, stunning as always in an all-black pant-suit. I notice that her hair is pulled into an uncommonly tamed bun. Even though she and Mia are entrenched in an animated conversation, she instantly looks up, as if through some unseen force, she senses my presence. Always...we seem to have that effect on each other. The smile she gives is genuine. I smile back, yet I don't go to her. There will be no trouble from me tonight.

This is where we are...the acceptance of this uneasy truce as our new reality. I don't have any clue as to how long this farce will actually last, but I'll play along for now. I don't have a choice if I hope to one day move beyond this point. Because that's exactly what I want to happen; I want to get her back in my life...forever. Not as a friend...as my lover.

Tonight...that estranged moment with Sarai, confirmed that I can't continue to live this lie. Although I have honestly tried, I can't be who she needs me to be. My mind isn't with her...my heart isn't with her. I tried...but ultimately, I failed.

When I went back to D.C. it should have been to formally dissolve my marriage with Sarai. What was I thinking? How could I ever believe that the ghost of "us" wouldn't haunt my days and wreak havoc on my nights? I know now that I will never have peace as long as she is somewhere in the universe...being loved by someone else. I know it every time I see her...every time we engage in conversation...every time she is merely in my presence.

Cosmic.

The only word righteous enough to describe our energy...our connection. It's as if our spirits are organically and soundly synched. There's no way I can walk away from that. Even if that means hurting Sarai...losing Kyle. I can't do it.

I just have to figure out how to get her on the same page.

At least she loves me. That was the hardest part...wondering if her feelings still existed on the level they once did. If I have learned anything over the past weeks, months...it's that she loves me just as fiercely as the day I walked out of her door. She may not speak the words out loud...but I know her. It's in the way she responds, the darkness of her eyes when she looks at me. I foolishly walked away from that kind of love once and I won't make that mistake again.

*****

I spot Kyle at the bar getting a drink. When he sees me he turns back to the bartender, I'm sure ordering something for me.

"What's up man?" We shake hands as I close in.

"What's up man of the hour" He greets me.

I laugh. "Not tonight my brother."

There are at least eight artists, including myself, who have works on display. A portion of the proceeds will go to local charities and scholarships. Tonight should be interesting with the complex mix of Besa's high end clientele and the creative coffeehouse crowd that Muse attracts, coming together for one common purpose. If nothing else, the night should be fun and certainly profitable.

The bartender reaches around Kyle to hand me the drink. The first burn settles in my belly as I take a minute to scan the room. The décor is more elegant than it was even on the night of the poetry showcase. It's amazing how the entire concept of a space can be reconfigured with a few simplistic changes.

"Our girl did well." Toni being the obvious point of reference.

"Yeah...she did." I respond without bothering to look in his direction. There is a measure of pride I feel in Toni's continued success. In truth, I am a lucky man. Undeservingly so. Sarai and Toni are as different as the moon and sun, but they are both amazing women. Most men would feel incredibly blessed having the opportunity to love...be loved...by either one. In my world, there's been the pleasure of sharing my life with both. Blessed...yet, cursed at the same damn time.

"How's work?" I ask, purposefully deflecting from the topic of "her".

"Busy as always. In fact, I have trials coming up this week so I can't stay long. One of my clients, Jade, is actually performing tonight. Have you heard of her?"

The name is vaguely familiar. "Wait, is she the pop singer who just got arrested?"

He shakes his head in apparent exasperation. "Exactly. That's why I have her performing tonight. I'm trying to do some damage control. In fact, I need to talk to Sarai about taking her on with The Paul Agency. Jade is talented, but that talent will be wasted if she can't get her head on straight. Right now she's a PR nightmare. I've got to get a dream team on board to help me revamp her image."

"Well Sarai and Marcus are certainly that...oh and Rae. God, that still catches me off-guard. Rae working for Sarai? How crazy is that?"

"Oh the tangled webs we weave...," he quotes.

Yes indeed my brother.

"Where is Sarai anyway?," he asks. I check my watch. "She and Marcus are coming over from the office. Don't worry; you know she'll get here just in time for the red carpet." We both find humor in the slightly offensive jab.

Social interruptions cause our conversation to cease. As always Kyle's mere presence garners lots of attention. I'm proud of him...of both of us really. Although we have chosen different paths, we are now both on the verge of living out our dreams. The unfortunate part of the story is that both of us envision our dream lives with the same woman.

Tangled webs.

I finish my drink and decide it's time to fulfill my networking obligations. The socializing aspect of business has never been my wheel-house, but I'm quickly learning that it's a necessary element. Kyle had shifted to the end of the bar but has now returned to claim his vacated seat.

"Hey man, I'm going to make my rounds before Besa finds me. I'll catch up with you later."

Instead of responding he remains silent. The once jovial mood is suddenly transformed. His face now bears the mark of strain. It's obvious that he wants to say something, but he seems unsure of how to proceed. I wait, giving him time to collect his thoughts. Of course the only source of tension in our lives right now revolves around Toni so I can only guess what's on his mind.

"Keenan, we need to talk." It's more of a command than a request.

I'm not used to this heaviness between us. There was a time when our relationship was easy. I yearn for those times...when he was simply my best friend and not my foe. This situation has mentally drained me and it's too exhausting to feign ignorance.

"When you're ready...I'm here."

*****

The event is now in full swing. Besa arrives and ushers all of the artists out to seduce the cameras. The onslaught of attention is intrusive, yet, exciting. It's hard to believe...two short years ago, I walked away from my corporate nine-to-five with nothing more than a seemingly impossible dream and lifetime of built-up passion. Then, I honestly didn't know if I could find success as an artist. I still can't believe how my life has come full circle...how close it is to being...perfect.

Almost.

I watch her from afar as she mingles and laughs with the usual crew: Dawn, Rae, Mia...and even Jamie. The realization hits me...I want to be a part of their inner circle. I want to be her other half...her plus one at social gatherings.

"She is a beautiful woman." The voice comes from behind me, and there is no mistaking the seductive lilt.

"Hello Besa." I greet my ever-observant business partner. She is a stunning sight in a vibrant red dress that clings to every inch of her curves. Her luxurious dark curls cascade down her back and her signature crimson lipstick perfectly complements her flawless, olive skin.

"Hello Mr. Jackson."

"So," she starts again without missing a beat. "Are you just going to stand here staring at her all night?" I have to appreciate her boldness, even though I should be angry at her for being in my business.

"Besa, Besa, Besa...don't you have business to attend to other than mine?"

"Mr. Jackson, in case you haven't figured it out, your business is my business sir. Besides, with the money I've made you, I deserve that privilege at least," she teases me.

She has indeed made good on her promise...nevertheless, she is by no means correct on her perspective about my life. Those two things I keep separate...on purpose.

"Ok, ok," she finally states after getting the hint that any discussion of Toni is off-limits. "You want to change the subject, yes? What about tonight? Are you enjoying...this?" With dramatic flair, she sweeps her hand around the spacious room.

"Yes," This time I answer with conviction. "This, Besa...is incredible. Thank you."

Before we can delve deeper into conversation a gentleman gets her attention and beckons her over.

"Ah well Mr. Jackson, if money calls...I must answer huh?" She laughs and raises her glass as she purposefully slinks off. I, in turn, go off in search of my wife, who I find with Marcus and Kyle in a corner near the stage. She only nods when she sees me and I simply nod back. There is a strange look on Kyle's face, as he watches us closely, but he doesn't say anything.

I'm done pretending.

Mia takes the stage and introduces Jade, the artist Kyle mentioned earlier. From the first note, it's evident that he did not exaggerate her level of talent. Reminiscent of a young Etta James, her breathy voice fills the room. As the final notes of the song fades, thunderous applause erupts. There is a certain look exchanged between Sarai and Marcus, and I am confident that Jade has indeed found her team.

After the performance, Kyle excuses himself to leave for the office. He grabs my attention on his way out of the door.

"Let's have that talk soon man."

"Indeed." I answer without flinching. The sooner I can stop living this lie, the better.

Once again, I find solace at the bar. Just as I order, I receive a notification on my phone. It is a text from Sarai saying that she and Marcus are going back to the office to finish up a report. She doesn't bother finding me to say good-bye. Maybe she's reached the point where she's done pretending too.

My eyes deliberately scan the room. I find her...and she is watching me. In the past she would have shied away. She doesn't look away tonight. Her dark eyes seem to penetrate the soul of me. Speak to me in ways that no other woman ever has. I raise my drink in acknowledgement. A seductive smile plays on her beautiful lips before she does the same.

I hear you.

*****

At last, the night is over and I can say with a great deal of certainty that it was a success. Still, it was increasingly difficult to enjoy it when I had to spend the entire night

187

avoiding Keenan and Sarai. The last thing I needed was for trouble to find me.

There was a time I once believed that we could do this...that we could co-exist on friendly terms. The moment we kissed, I knew that I had been premature and naïve in my thoughts. There is no escaping the chemistry we have...that unrecognizable force that always seems to drag us in the same direction. It's exhausting, trying to constantly fight it.

It proved difficult occupying the same space. There were times when I caught him watching me...other moments when he caught me watching him. We never looked away, just silently acknowledged each other's presence. Once, I felt the light caress of fingertips on the back of my neck. Shivers erupted throughout my body. Stolen glances, forbidden touches...too much for me to handle. This mental game of cat and mouse is taking its toll.

We are the last people remaining: me, Daniel, Tanya. The champagne flows freely as we celebrate our success and strategically contemplate the future.

"So," Daniel begins. "Let me be the first to say congratulations. If you ladies have any doubts remaining about expanding, I hope tonight eased some of your fears." Tanya nods in a show of affirmation. I raise my glass, confirming that I too am on board with our new venture.

"Finally!" Daniel exclaims. He has a right to his excitement. For months, I've been relentlessly holding on to my reins of control, but after tonight, I accept the vision and the plan for what we can build together, even beyond Muse.

"Ok, I get it. Where do we go from here though Daniel? How does this work?"

It is clear that he has worked out every detail of the intricate process. As we all initially agreed, Muse, in its original state and location will remain where it is. There is no doubt that it will remain profitable with the continuous stream of college students as its base clientele. Muse II, or whatever the final name that we decide upon, will be located further uptown. The venue will be larger, opening the door for more profitable events on a grander scale.

There is a question that has plagued me since the first moment we discussed the possibility of opening a new location. How are we going to pay for this project? We opened the doors of Muse with our own personal savings and a huge investment from EBS Ventures, Daniel's investment group. Muse has been profitable, but I'm not keen on the idea of borrowing money against its earnings. After coming so far, that is a financial risk I'm not willing to take.

"How do we pay for this?" I ask aloud with caution. Tanya speaks up as well. "Yes Daniel, let's please address that because as much as I'm all in favor of this project, I can't afford to put my kid's financial future at stake."

Daniel loosens his tie and pours himself another glass of champagne. For the first time I see signs of concern.

"Obviously, this is a huge financial under-taking. I've been researching and meeting with other investments groups to see if we can pull one of them in."

Another investment group? This news concerns me. The more hands in the pot, the less control me and Tanya retain.

"Another group?" I give voice to my fears. "That can't be the only way Daniel. EBS is already a partner. How much ownership is the new group going to want?"

He takes note of our fears and concerns and does his best to assuage them.

"Look, hear me out. We need to get the expansion up and running while we have momentum. I suggest getting this done in three to four months. In order to do that, we're going to need money...more money than EBS can commit to. Bringing in another partner only makes financial sense. You know me though. You know I won't do anything to put Muse or the project in jeopardy."

Tanya, it seems, is already sold. "I have to say Toni, this works for me. I mean, initially we were leery about partnering with EBS, but that has worked to our advantage. I suggest we let Daniel continue his research and we set another meeting to discuss his findings. We can make a sound decision then."

We all agree to call it a night with an understanding that conversations will resume at a date and time sometime in the near future. Exhaustion has set it, and my brain can't make much sense of it all anyway. Since I live closer than either of them, I volunteer to close shop. Wisely, they call an Uber and leave their vehicles in the parking lot. Just as I enter the office, my phone rings. My first guess is that it must be Kyle, checking in.

It is Besa.

"Hello bonita, I am sorry that I did not get a chance to speak with you before I left tonight."

"Hi Besa." I can't imagine why she is calling me. I assumed she would follow up with Daniel after tonight's event.

"Are you looking for Daniel?" I question, hurriedly gathering my personal belongings. "He's already left for the night."

"No, no I'm not. I am actually looking for you. Are you still at Muse?"

Her usual allure has worn thin. I'm too exhausted to figure out her games.

"Yes, Besa, I am. Look, I'm not trying to be rude, but what exactly do you need? I'm trying to finish up so that I can leave."

Somehow she finds amusement in my dilemma. "Well I won't keep you. Just make sure to check your office before you leave. I had one of my staff leave a gift for you. You can thank me later, love. Good-night."

The line goes dead before I can make sense of what she is saying. A gift? With guarded interest, I look around the office and notice a canvas against the far wall, covered by a black tarp. I approach it with caution, not sure of Besa's intentions. When I remove the tarp I am stunned to come face to face with my own reflection.

Damn Keenan.

Chapter 20: Silence

Leaning against the back door, I feel lost in a haze of emotions. The rain has come; its mist has covered the pane in a steamy shroud. There's nothing visible but distant lights beyond the bleak skies.

Earlier in the night I had promised Kyle that I would come over after the fundraiser. Instead, I exaggerated a headache to keep from going over. Not that my excuse was far from the truth. A state of complete weariness has indeed seeped into every inch of my bones. It seems that every time we find a good place, something with Keenan comes up to mess with my head. I can't keep doing this...but I can't seem to figure out how to get off of this emotional roller coaster.

While seeing him at Muse for the first time made me a wreck...seeing his painting tonight has made me a complete disaster. I haven't been able to shake it...that vision of myself on his canvas... half-naked, vulnerable...exposed...illuminated.

He loves me.

Anyone who ever lays their eyes on *that* would know it. The way he captured the early morning light against my skin...the way he captured my wild curls around my sleeping, exhausted face. He exposed himself...exposed the rawness of his feelings. No inhibitions or restraints.

My heart is being shattered all over again. I miss him. I miss him loving me like *that*. I miss him leaving me in a tangled mass of sheets...satiated...spent. It's why I've had such a difficult time letting him go. I never wanted to lose...*that*.

I trek to the kitchen for a second cup of coffee...attempting to clear the fog of confusion from my head.

Silly girl.

I can't spend the rest of my life longing for a man who lives another life. The lyrics from Erykah Badu's "See you next lifetime" plays through mind. Next time Keenan, is my somber thought. Maybe, somehow our spirits will reconnect in another life...and maybe then we'll get it exactly right.

The doorbell rings just as I am about to alleviate my tensions with a warm, relaxing lavender-filled bath. I pray it's not Kyle coming over against my wishes; however, the second ring never comes. With caution, I approach the door and peep through the keyhole to identify my intruder. My breath catches in my throat. This is absolutely the last thing I need.

Or maybe... it is everything I've wanted.

The door is open, and once again Keenan Jackson is allowed entrance into my crumbling world. I step aside without saying a word...too tired to even question his presence. I settle in on the chaise...and wait. He closes the door behind him and without prompting, settles into the nearest chair facing me.

Silence.

Under any other circumstances, this void would be considered awkward; but we are familiar. And in our familiarity, we find some level of comfort.

The room cloaks our expressions in semi-darkness. The rain drowns our thoughts with its constant patter. Our old friend Donny Hathaway serenades us with his soulful rhythms.

Silence.

Who needs words when bodies are familiar? When there are longing gazes across the space of rooms...when the faint echoes of heartbeats become synched on one accord. Even in silence my body speaks to him. Does he recognize the subtle arch of my back? Or perhaps he detects the shift in my breaths. Whatever the cause, he responds...and without resignation...

I finally welcome him home.

Somehow...even in the midst of our silence... we have concluded that we are simply too exhausted to continue this fight. He comes to me...and I embrace him with arms wide open.

He lay down next to me on the chaise and I instantly fold my frame into the curve of his back. Eagerly, I snatch the band from his hair, allowing his snake-like dreads to escape. I bury my hands and face in his long coils...breathe in the scent of him. There it is...that familiar stirring in the pit of my belly.

I have missed this man.

Slowly I massage his scalp, feeling the tension release from his rigid shoulders. At any point he can stop me, but he doesn't.

We will no longer fight.

Silence.

Who needs words when there are butterfly touches...simple caresses that awaken long buried cravings?

I draw his shirt over his head...trace his naked back with my fingertips down to his belted waist. His body reacts. His breaths become ragged in expectation. My own ache intensifies, but I want to savor every minute of this stolen, impulsive moment. I reach around his slim waist...tease the soft hairs of his belly. His heated skin quivers beneath my fingers.

I begin to unbuckle his belt. Deft fingers now tremble in anticipation of seeing him...loving him. For a brief moment he steadies my hand with his own before assisting me in removing what remains of his clothing. Tears spring to my eyes and spill over onto my cheeks.

My god, he is beautiful.

As I remembered, his body is sculpted perfection from head to toe. His smooth cocoa skin gleams with a fine sheen of sweat. His now erect penis is swollen...enlarged...hungry. I reach for him...just wanting to touch him...commit the feel of him to memory.

Silence.

Who needs words when there are sensual kisses? Kisses that savor the taste of forbidden desires. My mouth replaces my hands. I just need to taste him...want to feel his engorged heat along the length of my tongue...taste the lingering traces of salty skin across my lips. His hands become entangled in my hair as I entice him with my mouth. Pulling...caressing...sucking...nibbling...pulling. Our erotic dance almost breaks him.

Almost.

Silence... broken only by his sudden, harsh cries of pleasure. No words yet escape our lips.

I break away...hurriedly removing my clothing...needing desperately to quench the ache that now threatens to overwhelm me. I stand before him... as naked and exposed as his recreated image on canvas. His smoldering eyes are dark, wild with lust. I could allow him to take me. In his state of raw hunger he could fuck me into submission. But I don't want that.

This time, I want to have the advantage. He calls for me...and I answer.

Silence

Broken only by hoarse cries of unbridled passion as I take all of him into all of me. We cling to each other as our bodies remember their long-forgotten rhythms. I drench him in my erupting juices...clench him in spasms as my inner walls once again became acquainted with his penetrating strokes. We cry together as his succulent lips attack my waiting mouth...the flavor of each other's love lingers on our tongues. In this moment there is no denying who truly owns me. He claims places no other man has ever reached...not even Kyle. Together we rock until I feel the first tremors of orgasm.

Silence.

Broken only by me screaming his name as I explode...him moaning mine as he erupts. Emotionally and physically spent, I collapse against his drenched chest. The powerful echo of his heartbeat resonates in my ear. I want to speak...to find the words to adequately describe my emotions...but...no words can do justice to what our bodies have experienced. Instead, I rub my face against the matted hairs of his chest.; bathe in the intoxicating blend of sweat and juices. I just want to commit to memory the element of 'us'.

There are no words spoken...no false promises of tomorrow...just the beautiful gift of this silent moment.

Chapter 21: Afterglow

We lay together for hours, wrapped in our love, not caring about the reality of life beyond these walls. Our skin holds conversations that our mouths are too shy to speak. Can't speak...for fear of shattering the illusion. Our limbs just as entangled as the lies we've woven. There is a surprising lack of shame from my perspective. Maybe because I've finally come to the realization that I need this man...want him. Even if that means that "having" him means a life of stolen moments and secret whispers.

I want him.

Exactly when this transformation occurred, I'm not sure. When did I become this woman who would accept a man under these terms? This woman...I don't recognize her. Then again, I've never loved anyone as righteously as I love Keenan. No longer in denial, I accept that our connection is more than physical. Our spirits are aligned in ways that are beyond complimentary. It is why, as we lay here now, I breathe in his breath as naturally as I breathe my own.

He is awake even though his eyes are closed. Even though his body is still, his fingers playfully grip my tangled hair and trace my neckline. I am spent from our hours of lovemaking, yet, my body still responds to his simple touch.

I watch him at rest: full, delicious lips, glowing chocolate skin, dreads hanging to the middle of his back.

Perfection.

After some length, he opens his eyes and lovingly gazes at me with a smile on his face.

"Hey you."

My heart is happy. I didn't know how he would feel...after. Would his heart be full of regret, remorse? His smile though, the sincerity on his face, lets me know that he has no regrets about loving me.

"Hey back." I whisper, matching his smile with one of my own.

My heart is full, overflowing with emotions. It is not my intention to ruin this moment but I don't want to hold back. One thing about stolen moments, you never know when or if the next one will come.

"I love you."

He stares at before leaning down to kiss me fully on the lips.

"I know baby...I love you too."

His declaration leaves me in an embarrassed state of satisfaction. In reality there is nothing right about this...but here...in this space...it is everything we need.

I kiss him back with force...a passionate and personal transference of emotions. As our lips and tongues search for each other, the ache in the pit of my stomach grows in intensity. My hands move from his hair to claw desperately at his back. I pull him into me, molding our outstretched bodies together. His body is still slick with sweat from our last encounter. I break away, gasping for air. He takes the reprieve as an opportunity to attack my neck...sucking and biting in a rebellious attempt to mark his territory. I am losing myself in the feel of him. His wild dreads brush against my skin, the sensation like erotic feathers...tantalizing...teasing. He grips me firmly and rolls on top of me. Grabbing my face, he forces me to look into his eyes, now clouded with passion. He kisses me with unbridled hunger as I wrap strands of his hair tautly around my hands...preparing for this ride.

"Toni," My name...a sweet seductive whisper against my own mouth.

"Yes," I answer in a quivering breath.

He grabs my ass and forcefully enters my wet canal. I cry out as his thickness fills me completely. "I love you." He pulls back and forcefully rams again...claiming my body as only he can. "I love you...I love you...I love you." The repetition of his affirmations and strokes are more than I can handle. I can't hold on. My forceful orgasm showers him in my love. I cling to him...our bodies methodically rocking until his own journey is complete. He buries his face in my neck; I bury my own in his hair.

We are motionless...still...even as night turns to day and the brilliance of dawn envelops us. Still we lay...clinging, holding, grasping...bound by the spell of the moment.

Until...somewhere in the midst of our discarded clothing...his phone begins to ring.

Chapter 22: Broken Promises

The day is dark. Although it is early morning, the storm has brought forth gray skies. At least there is now a reprieve from the relentless rain. I'm learning that these southern storms are often unpredictable.

My heart is incredibly heavy...held hostage by the weight of realizations. My marriage to Keenan is over.

I should have listened. His doubt...his insecurity regarding his own feelings...was loud even without words. Instead, I was lost in my own self-imposed blindness. All along, he knew that coming here would be his biggest failure. And now...now my marriage is over. Yeah...it is definitely over.

I believe that if I say it to myself over and over it will finally soak into my brain and trickle down into my heart. If my heart gets the message, then maybe, when the words are finally said out loud...it won't hurt as much. Perhaps that's wishful thinking, but right now, it's all that I have to hold on to. I can only try to minimize the eventual agony to come. In truth, I can't stop it from coming. My marriage is over...yeah...it is definitely over.

And my heart is heavy with that knowledge.

I knew it the moment I walked into the house last night. After a quick appearance at the fundraiser, I decided to go into the office, which wasn't an unusual occurrence since the grand opening. Business has been overwhelming, which has called for early mornings and late nights...unfortunately not in the bedroom. We have barely been able to keep up. Although I hate to admit it, and I would never say it out loud, hiring Rayna...Rae...was the best thing that Marcus could have done. She's incredibly smart, and doesn't mind getting her hands dirty. She's done everything...copying, filing, and meeting with clients...all without complaint. Honestly, if it wasn't for her relationship with Toni, I would take her under my wings to mentor her. But...there's that relationship. And now...yeah especially now with recent events, I am not trying to have anything to do with anyone linked to Toni.

I came home to an empty house. Empty, cold and void of warmth and light. There was no television, no music... all indications that my dear husband hadn't been home for hours. Granted, he could have gotten caught up in a meeting with Besa, but my instincts don't entertain that thought. No, when I walked in, I knew immediately where his ass was...somewhere with...her.

Damn.

Women, we rely heavily on our instincts...those internal radars which alert us whenever something is just not right. Everything in me was screaming that this...this was not right. As soon as I got settled, I called him. My hands were shaking. My heart wanted so badly for him to answer the phone, but my mind already knew that he wouldn't.

So I grabbed a bottle of wine and waited.

But that mother fucker never came home. I don't know how much time passed before I finally fell asleep on the sofa. Times like this I wish I had a really good girlfriend to call on, someone who would have taken me to Toni's house to raise holy hell. That's not my reality though. I've always been too busy working to make friends. Plus, my mother always instilled in me to never put my faith in females or males either for that fact. I laugh to myself as that random thought crosses my mind...fantastic advice Mother.

The tears won't stop falling. Not from weakness, but from pure anger. How could you Keenan? Really, how could you do this to me yet again? I just wanted him to have faith in us...be strong enough for us. Apparently that was too much to ask.

I close my eyes and press my fingers to my throbbing temples. The chastising tone of my mother's voice echoes in my ear. "You are a damn fool Sarai." Yeah I was...I was a damn fool for bringing him here. It's too late to change that. The damage has been done. So what does this fool do now?

I know what I want to do. I want to call Kyle. I want to fuck up her shit like she's fucking up mine. I want everyone involved in this mess to hurt just as much as I hurt right now. I want to call him and ask him where the fuck his woman is right now.

But...there is still a part of me that wants to believe that he's not with her.

I am so angry. I hate being this angry without being able to direct it at the cause. I had plans for today...plans for us. I took a much needed day off so that we could spend some quality time together...reconnect in a way that has been lacking. Instead...I'm wasting my time, miserably sitting at this table waiting on my husband to come into his own house like a thief in the night.

All morning I wait. He still doesn't answer his phone. I have left a number of irate, hateful messages. It never crosses my mind that he's not ok. That maybe he is crashed in a ditch somewhere, a victim of Atlanta's rained out, oiled slicked roads. I never have that feeling. I know that it isn't a car crash that's keeping him from coming home.

It is *her*.

I'm back at the kitchen table, back to my bottle of wine, when I finally hear the key in the lock. I move to stand in front of the door. My entire body is vibrating in anger and...disgust. Who is he to make a fool out of me?

My husband walks in our house and as soon as he sees me, he drops his head in shame. I lose it. I scream, cry, hit, punch...anything to connect, to cause actual damage.

"Motherfucker! Who the hell are you to make a fool out of me? How dare you? How dare you Keenan? How dare you walk into our house after being with her all night? She's not your wife! How could you?!"

I want to hurt him physically as much as he has hurt me emotionally...mentally. It is one thing to know that he had slept with someone while we were separated...when things between us were uncertain, but to discover that he is sleeping with her now...*now*. *Now* he's supposed to just be my husband.

Two words. Two words...so common in their simplicity...yet two words confirm my deepest fears.

"I'm sorry."

"Sorry? Sorry, Keenan? You're sorry? You didn't last four months in this damn city before you end up in her bed? Before you disrespect me, our vows...our family? You are more than sorry. You are pathetic and you are a coward. You...are not worth *me*."

I crumble to the floor. Cried out, spent from our emotional baggage...so heavy from the weight of it all. I wanted so badly to be wrong. I needed to be wrong. Even in the midst of disaster...I love him. I love my husband and I need him to love me back. I need him to not love someone else. I need for him to reassure me that this is just some nightmare that I would soon wake from...reassure me that we are fixable.

"Sarai." He dares speak my name in the softest whisper, belying his malicious act. "Sarai, I am so sorry. I swear to God, I never meant to hurt you. I couldn't...I failed...I couldn't stay away."

Slowly, I raise my head from my arms and watch him. Anger is no longer my unwanted companion. Only weariness remains. I'm sure my laughter is void of humor.

"You didn't even try."

He doesn't respond. He can't... because in his heart he knows that I am telling the truth. He didn't even try. *Sarai, Sarai, Sarai...you foolish woman...you brought him back to the lioness' den and he realized that he never stopped loving her.*

"You love her that much that you would sacrifice *everything?* Everything we have spent our entire lives building? This is not *Love Jones* or some other movie Keenan." My voice chokes with emotion. "This is our *life.*"

He runs his hands over his face. A gesture typically reserved for moments of angst or frustration. It breaks my heart to think that she knows that about him...those little nuances that made him familiar only to me.

He looks directly at me, wavering not in the least.

"Yes...I love her that much."

There it is...the undeniable truth...my husband...absolutely, completely in love with someone else.

"I tried to deny it for a long time. I came home. I came back to you...but I...I can't do this. I can't live this lie. I'm so sorry for that."

Who is this man in my presence? My entire concept of who he is has been shattered. It dawns on me that I have been holding on to a dream that has been long gone. This...this isn't what I had planned for my life...this empty shell of a marriage. What exactly am I trying to hold on to? Truthfully, we haven't been on the same page in a long time. At some point he changed into a man that no longer resembled my husband. His dreams became different...his goals, different. I tried to hold on to the young man I fell in love with as a young girl. But we're not young anymore and we have grown into people who are merely shells of our former selves. And I...I am the only one holding on.

No more...no more Sarai. If he wants out, then I will let him go.

I wipe my face...straighten my shoulders...attempt to regain what little dignity I have left. With newfound purpose, I open the door. I am done yelling...done begging.

Done.

His face is full of sorrow. "Sarai." I can hear the plea in his voice. Not a plea to stay, to work things out, to make our family whole. No. It is the plea of a man who wants forgiveness for his sins.

He won't get that today.

Blankly I stare through him. I have no other words for this man.

He never whispers my name again. A long sigh escapes his lips before he walks out of the door. As soon as he crosses the threshold, I slam the door behind him. Numbness invades my entire body. My movements are strictly automatic as I casually walk to the fridge, get another bottle of wine and refill my glass.

My thoughts drift to Toni, the woman responsible for this chaos. I warned her, but she didn't heed my warning. The first time...she didn't know the damage she was causing. *That was then.* Now, she willingly stepped into my house and broke my family. Somehow, she would have to answer for that.

Outside, the rain has come. The dark clouds have closed off any remnants of sunshine.

The broken promises of a new day quickly fade into a foreboding haze of gray.

Chapter 23: Pieces

Agony. That's the only way to describe what I am feeling right now. Pure agony. I anxiously sip on my fresh brewed cup of coffee while waiting for Kyle. I try to calm my mind, but so far, that has been a complete fail. I've thought of a thousand ways to keep this as painless as possible, however, I've since come to the conclusion that to do that would be an impossible task. How can I tell Kyle that I no longer love him without breaking his heart? How will I tell him that his greatest fear is coming true...that I am choosing Keenan? How can I look him in the face and tell him that?

The ceaseless ringing of the phone brought reality rushing back to us. For a few stolen hours we were lost in our own world. The darkness aided in secluding us in our own selfish haven of love. The ringing broke the spell of the moment...a moment that I wasn't ready to end.

He moved to answer it. He should have. In that moment there was a choice to be made. Answer...lie...betray....or, don't and choose to stay with me, ultimately, sealing the fate of his marriage. He shifted...and I became afraid. Selfishly, I put my hand on the small of his back. His muscles relaxed... he stayed.

I exhaled and rested against his back. *He chose me.* Even if for only this moment...he chose me.

Night turned to dawn...dawn turned into the beaming light of day. Still...he was here. Coffee...breakfast...*he remained.* We took a long hot bath reveling in each other's skin...tastes.

He remained.

At some point, he left. We couldn't hide away forever. I called him an Uber and while we waited, we stood in the middle of my living room...embracing each other...inhaling each other...reminiscent of that first night together many moons ago. I knew then that he would be trouble and he had has certainly given life to my theory.

There was no discussion on what would happen now. I don't know what he will do on his end...how he will clean up his own mess. All I know is that today I will lose my best friend...and I will have to live with that choice.

I have to tell Kyle. I won't do that to him. I owe him so much more than what he's getting from me right now...this half-hearted attempt at love. He deserves better...he deserves the truth. No matter the cost...he deserves the truth.

Life can be so complicated; choices, can be so complicated. So many crazy...fucked up decisions that impact the totality of our lives. For as long as I can remember, I've always needed Kyle...and somewhere hidden in the crevices of my mind, I've always known that he's always wanted me. Kyle has always been in my corner...even the days when I have been at my worst...he's always been there. Today though...today I say goodbye to my friend. I can only hope that this great sacrifice will be worth it in the end.

Please Keenan be worth it.

The doorbell rings. I wait. After a minute, it rings again. My grip tightens on the handle of my coffee mug as I hear his key unlock the door.

"Hey babe." He lovingly greets me, fully entering the room.

God, what would my life be without the comfort of his presence?

He looks good, as usual. A polo style shirt with khaki pants...casual, still, so good. I don't move to greet him. I can barely muster a "hey" back as he smiles at me, walking towards the sofa. He sits down, leans his head back and stretches his long legs in front of him.

The weariness escapes his body in one drawn-out sigh. Before he can get too comfortable I ask about his day. I have not spoken to him since early yesterday. He has been incredibly busy with trials.

Without opening his eyes he gives me a run-down of the past twenty-four hours. Truthfully, I am only half listening. My nerves are getting the best of me. He abruptly stops talking and looks at me.

"You know what...enough with all of the boring stuff. I am officially done working for the entire weekend. What's going on with you? You want to go out tonight or stay in? I'm good either way."

He waits for an answer; however, no words can bypass the huge lump that has formed in my throat. I can only stare back. He senses that something is different...wrong. He's always been perceptive.

"You ok?" There is a measure of concern in his voice. "What's going on Toni?"

"We need to talk Kyle."

There are a thousand questions in his eyes. I shy away from his penetrating gaze.

"Ok. What exactly do we need to talk about?"

I'm not sure how to proceed...but I can't drag this out forever. Once the words are out of my mouth I know that I will never be able to take them back.

"I slept with Keenan."

Done.

The words are in the atmosphere. Let the consequences commence. He stares at me for a long time as if he is still trying to process my words. He starts to speak, then suddenly stops. I want to explain, but I know it will be useless. Kyle, as an attorney is used to filtering through bs. No matter how sincere I am, he will take it as exactly that.

"You...you slept...with Keenan?" It is a rhetorical question so I don't say it again. He sits upright, looking as if the weight of the world has come crashing down on his shoulders. My sense of guilt seems to swallow me whole. Ashamed, I stare into my now cold cup of coffee. My hands are shaking.

"Toni, look at me...you're honestly telling me that you slept with Keenan? *You slept with him?*"

"Yes. I slept with him Kyle. I'm so sorry. I'm so sorry for hurting you, for doing this to us. I'm...I'm sorry."

He stands and begins to furiously pace across the floor. His pained face is set in anger and hurt. In fact, for as long as we've been friends I've never seen this much pain emanate from him before. Well only once...when his mother died. To think of that pain as my only rival, makes me sick to my stomach. This can never be made right.

"When?"

His legal instincts need to know the details, need to piece together the story from beginning to end.

I know better.

"You don't want to know that Kyle. You only think you do."

Now the anger comes. "No! You don't get to do this. You don't get to dictate how I handle all this bullshit you're throwing at me. Tell me when."

I resign. "Last night."

"Last...night? he chokes on the words. "Where?"

More. He wants more. Instead of answering, my eyes travel around the room then back to his face.

"Here Toni? You let him come back here?" Still I can't answer. What exactly am I supposed to say?

He laughs, but it's almost sadistic in nature. When he looks back at me there is fire in his eyes. I can feel myself shrinking under the intensity of his gaze.

"What was I thinking? How did I think that for once in your life you would do the right thing and put me first? Toni does it even matter to you that he didn't choose you? He had the opportunity to choose you and he didn't. Are you so broken...that you would take second hand love over something *real?* Do you even know how *pathetic* that is*?*"

A swell of tears floods my face. Never has Kyle spoken to me in the manner in which he is now. His words are daggers piercing the deepest part of being.

"It...is *real* though Kyle," I plea, "It's always been real. I love you...but I can't love you like I love him. I tried. I never intended to hurt you."

"How is that fair Toni? What about this is fair? I've been here all along. I...never...left! I picked up and put together all of the broken pieces of *you*...did you forget that? Did you forget the tears you cried over him? Did you forget not being able to get out of bed? How could you forget me? When you slept with him last night...how could you forget *me?*"

He sat back on the sofa and put his head in his hands.

Tears.

Oh my God, what have I done?

I go to him. As I've done on so many other occasions, I sit on the floor and put my head in his lap.

"Kyle I'm sorry. I'm so sorry. Don't hate me. Please don't hate me."

He buries his face in my hair...ends "us" in one sentence.

"No Toni I don't hate you...but I am sick and tired of loving you." With that he kisses me on the forehead and stands to leave. I attempt to grab his hand but he abruptly shakes me off and keeps walking.

"Kyle...please." I cry out to him in a desperate attempt to save some part of us. Still, he keeps walking. He stops at the door, only long enough to remove the spare key to my house from his keychain. Then he walks out without further words, leaving only the shattered remains of our friendship behind in his wake.

Chapter 24: Naked Mornings

I have fallen in love with mornings. There is something special about the early light of day. The way it glows across skies and surfaces; it is the promise of new beginnings. Even the ordinary seems magnificent...the magnificent seems...brilliant. In its vibrant light I love her the most.

This morning, like so many others that we have now shared, I sit watching her. My muse, come to life...my breath of inspiration. I no longer kid myself about that. How did I ever walk away from her? She has given me everything...sacrificed everything. For me...because she loves me that much. All within her that is light and love...she has transferred to me. Even when I've least deserved it. Now, I can finally give her the love back that she deserves.

Yes. Every morning brings a new set of promises. And I can't wait to see where this new journey will take us.

I'm glad that she is still. There have been many restless nights when she has awakened with nightmares. It has not been easy dealing with her heartbreak over Kyle. She loves him. Not the same love as she has for me...I'm confident in that now. His love was familiar...it was comfortable. She misses his love. Sometimes I feel so guilty for her sacrifice, but to have the ability to love her...well it's worth it.

I thought I could let her go. I thought I could live without her in my life...that I could live with her loving someone else. I have finally realized that when it comes to her I am a selfish man. I want to wake up every morning in this beautiful light and see her bathed in it. I never again want to deny myself the luxury of the sight of her wild tangled hair...the satin feel of her skin.

She stirs slightly before opening her eyes. She blinks as my face comes into focus. "Morning beautiful."

"Morning love." She smiles back at me.

She sits up and the sheet barely conceals her nakedness. Mindlessly, she pushes her out of control mane away from her face.

"Coffee." She simply commands and I laugh. A fresh pot is already brewing. In these ways we are familiar and I can now wholly enjoy these casual moments. I know she can't even begin to have a decent conversation until she's had at least one cup. And right now I need the full extent of her clarity because there are definitely conversations to be had.

I leave her side to head into the kitchen. Countless thoughts invade my head. This time around it will be different. There will be no pretense of salvaging a relationship between me and Sarai. That chapter of my life is over and it's time to take the steps to begin again. Until that can truly happen, there are matters to be resolved. Matters like my daughter...my pending divorce...Kyle.

Kyle.

Making this decision will potentially cause more grief than I imagined. My relationship with Kyle is irrevocably damaged. In the past, Kyle and I could get through any obstacles that came our way. Our bond was always strong enough. But this...I am not naïve enough to believe that we will get through this. I'm not exactly sure how I'll manage life without having him in it. In fact, if I think about it all long enough, hard enough, it would overwhelm my brain. So I've come to terms with the fact that facing this situation will be a day by day process.

When I return, she has already changed into shorts and a tank top. Even in her most casual state, she is beautiful. I want to forget the world and be lost in her for the day, but I gather all of the restraint I can muster to focus on the issues at hand.

"So," she begins, relieving me of a cup. "Where do we go from here Mr. Jackson?"

I take a long sip and gather my thoughts before answering. "I know we've had this conversation before, still, I want you to know that I'm in a different place. Toni, I love you. I want to be with you. From this day forward, I want to spend the rest of my days with you. I know that I've given you reason to doubt me, to not trust me, but I beg you to please be patient with me in this process. I just need a little time to get my affairs in order."

Her doubt is evident when she responds.

"As much as I want to believe you...believe *in* you, Keenan, I can't help thinking that you will not follow through. And just so you know, I didn't end things with Kyle just on the wishful thinking that we would be together. I just knew that it wouldn't be fair to be with him knowing that you and I had slept together. So if you're thinking that you owe me for that...don't. Come to me...be with me...only if that is exactly what you want to do."

She pauses and for a moment is lost in her own thoughts. Suddenly she reaches out and touches my face. I close my eyes and indulge in the feel of her soft caress.

"I'm...exhausted Keenan," she continues, "Loving you has exhausted all of my...everything. So I don't have time or the energy for the games, the fluctuating mentality, the dual lives...I can't do it. This absolutely has to be exactly what you want."

I move next to her on the bed...grab her face in my hands. "Toni, I promise you that I will make this happen. You don't have to rely on my words. Watch what happens. I will make this right."

I kiss her softly, enjoying the sweet taste of caramel mocha on her lips.

She stares at me before reaching out to tug at my dreads.

"Make it right Keenan."

Chapter 25: Broken

The ringing of the phone interrupts my thoughts. I completely ignore it. There is no need to see who it is. Regardless of the name illuminated on the display, I won't talk to them. Lately, I haven't been in the mood for talking. The past few weeks have been a blur. Honestly, I don't know how I managed to get through trial week, but I did. All I wanted was to stew in my unreleased anger, but I had to hold it together…to let my feelings take a backseat to my priorities. Keenan has taken everything from me. *Everything.* I couldn't allow him to impact my carefully orchestrated career.

Today, though, I am free to dwell in my feelings and I plan on taking full advantage of the given moment. The time has come for me to grieve…for everything. So many times today I've wanted to pick up the phone to call my mom…to talk this situation out…get some advice on how to move forward without the love of my life and my brother in name.

This situation has been a tremendous blow. I have lost my best friends. And now, in the midst of my sorrow I can't even call the one person who could always soothe my anguish with words and heal my wounds with kisses. Drunk on wine and buried in my somber thoughts, I sit with my head buried in my hands.

Fuck.

Maybe it wouldn't be so bad if I could at least call my father; however, things between us have been estranged since my mother's untimely death. I love my dad, but he's not an emotional man. According to his old-fashioned standards, a man handles whatever life throws at him with unshakeable strength...unfaltering courage. Even if it's the death of the woman you have loved for over 40 years. You don't cry, at least not that anyone knows. You don't fall to pieces. *No.* You bury your feelings six feet deep and you adorn them with roses.

Then, you walk away and move on.

Even if your only son with that woman is coming undone at the seams. You don't hug away his hurt. *For he's a man, and not a boy.* Instead, you encourage him to file away his best memories and get back to the business of creating new ones.

That man, I cannot call. That man can't know that his only son has failed his rigid test of manhood. This man is broken, crying, and once again coming undone.

I suppose at the end of the day I have only myself to blame. Much of my hurt stems from the knowledge that circumstances could have been different. I could have told her ages ago how I really felt. I should have. Now, it's too late. Her heart...every piece of her in fact, belongs to someone else.

To him.

The truth, if I must face it...is that I never stood a chance. I wanted so badly to believe that if I just loved her enough...if I showed her enough....if I held her enough...she would stay. Who knows... maybe she would have if fate hadn't dealt me the cruel hand of sending Keenan back to Atlanta. Even with all of our years of friendship, much less relationship, our love was not strong enough to compete with her love for him. How can I not hate him for that?

Yes, he is my brother, but I hate him for fucking up my life the way he has. Honestly, I don't think I will ever forgive him.

The doorbell rings. Not expecting anyone, I am beyond irritated at the intrusion. At first, I ignore it...willing whoever is on the other side of the door to go away. But there it is again, piercing through my wall of solitude. I am prepared to curse the unfortunate soul on the other side door when I snatch it open.

Sarai.

As horrible as I feel, she looks ten times worse. The last thing I want is to appease her depressed state of being; nevertheless, she is still my friend...my sister...although I'm sure that particular status is now in question. I step back and allow her entrance into my home. Once she is fully inside, I walk off, back towards the comfort of my sofa. She cautiously follows behind me...her steps tentative, as if she's unsure that being in my space is where she really wants to be.

As she settles into the comfort of one of my oversized chairs, I have another chance to really take in her appearance. Her brilliantly red hair is pulled back into a severe bun. Her pretty face is void of make-up. Fitted jeans, a gray hoodie, and light boots replace her usual suit. Not exactly the well put together Sarai that I have come to know and love.

I want to be angry. After all, she is as much to blame for this mess as Keenan. Still, I am all too aware of her pain. For all of her faults, there has never been any doubt of her love for Keenan. They just came to a fork in the road and each chose a different path.

"Wine?" I offer, holding up the near empty bottle. It is the second one that I have nursed throughout the day. She nods without speaking as I retrieve another glass and a freshly chilled bottle from the kitchen. I pour her a full glass before sufficiently replenishing my own.

I take a long sip and look in her direction... waiting. She begins to speak, but is suddenly overcome by an onslaught of tears. The old Kyle would've tried to comfort her. That task is too much for this Kyle. My own level of pain is already too much for me to bear. As much as I love her as a sister, I just don't have anything left to offer. Instead, I wait patiently until she regains some semblance of control.

"Why are you here Sarai?"

"Where else am I supposed to go Kyle?" Her piteous look tugs at my heart. "I couldn't stand another minute in that house. It's not a home. I don't have my daughter...my husband has pretty much abandoned me. I have no family here." Her voice breaks with emotion. "I didn't know what to do...where to go. I know I don't have a right to be here, but...I can't be alone right now."

I close my eyes. What is she expecting from me? Here I am, just as broken as she is. The old Kyle would have tried to fix, console, comfort...but man this Kyle...this Kyle is just emotionally worn out.

"What you need...want...I just don't have the capacity to give." Pausing, I take another long sip. "Sarai, I'm sorry. I want to be angry with you for bringing him back but...I did this. I convinced him to come to Atlanta...to find a new beginning. I convinced him to put distance between the two of you...convinced him that it was all in his best interests." I can't help but laugh as I think back to that fateful conversation. "Truthfully, my intentions were selfish. I had lost my mom and I just needed him to be...close. So I did this."

"Kyle, trust me, there's a pot full of blame to pass around." She laughs sarcastically, brushing her tears away with the back of her hands. "I mean really. You can't get more stupid than to drag your husband back to the woman he tells you he's in love with. How crazy is that shit? What was I thinking?"

"You thought your love would be enough."

Laughter once again turns into tears.

"Yeah I did. I thought I could love him enough Kyle. And you know what...I'm so...mad...that it wasn't enough. How could all of those years...our family...our daughter...how could that not be enough? How did we grow that far apart that I didn't even realize it wouldn't be enough?"

We sit in silence for moments...the stillness intermittently broken by her shallow breaths.

"I'm sorry for...this."

More silence.

"So what are you going to do?"

"I don't know. I really don't know what my next move is other than getting my daughter. Keenan's parents will be here in a few weeks. God, I don't know what to tell her...them. At this point I don't even know if I'll stay in Atlanta. I may just pack everything up and go back to D.C. Start over."

"Go back to D.C.? I thought the whole reason you were here was to manage the Atlanta branch of the agency. Why would you give up on that now?"

"I don't want to Kyle. I just need to figure everything out."

I move then to embrace her. As much as I am hurting, it's obvious that what I'm going through pales in comparison to her level of devastation. Her life has completely fallen apart...her family, torn apart.

She holds on to me, crying into the folds of my arms. My grief slowly evolves into anger. This is a fine mess that Keenan and Toni have made. What gives them the right to fuck up people's lives the way they have?

Anger evolves... into hate.

"I am so sorry Sarai. I promise you, we will find a way to make this right." For the first time since she entered my home, I see the fire reignite in her eyes.

"We will make this right."

Chapter 26: Sweetest Thing

Awakening from my deep slumber is proving to be a slow process. For the past ten days, I've been a slave to Muse. Business has been steadily increasing since the exhibit and we have barely been able to keep up.

After further discussion, we have decided that bringing in another partner only makes sound business sense. Although I am resigned to Muse's fate, I still have to admit that a part of me still harbors a sense of fear, especially knowing that a new firm will be involved. The only way I've found to combat that feeling is by staying focused on the end game....seeing Muse, my baby, grow to its full potential. So many years of sacrifice and hard work were, at long last, coming full circle.

Tanya is still on vacation, and while Mia has made herself more available, I still don't want to burn her out. I've practically been living in the back office which has created some distance between me and Keenan. Not exactly the way I pictured the start of our new life together, but at this point in the process, I can't see any way around it.

The house is dark, except for the play of shadows against the wall...silent, except for the haunting voice of Lauryn Hill resonating throughout the house. I venture beyond the confines of the room and pad barefoot down the hall in search of Keenan. I find him in my rarely used guest room. Since officially moving in I have allowed him to set up shop, at least until we make more permanent arrangements.

The room is in a total state of chaos. Large black tarps are spread out around the room to protect the expensive wooden floors beneath. Canvases of various sizes are either carelessly strewn about, leaning against walls or unfinished on easels. Standing in the middle of it all is the love of my life, staring blankly at one of those partially finished canvases. His hands, chest and face are smeared in a rainbow of colors. His only clothing: his well-worn paint-stained jeans. His dreads are carelessly pulled into a ponytail that hangs in long strands down his back. Before interrupting, I stand watching him. Moments like this are when I love him the most...when he is in his element, among the paints, oils, canvases, and brushes. Baring witness to his passion, focus, and intensity is incredibly sexy to me.

I cross the room and wordlessly wrap my arms around his naked waist...lean my face against his structured back. I love loving him and even under these less than ideal circumstances, loving him has been worth everything.

Since I first entered the room, he moves...unwrapping my arm and bringing my hand to his lips.

"Hey love."

"Hey back" I softly whisper. We are still for a long moment. Our coordinated breaths are the only sounds in the room other than Lauryn's silky tone.

Without warning, he pulls me around to face him. He stares at me with so much fire that it literally leaves me breathless and shivering. I search his face for some indication of his mood, which I know can vary throughout the day. His face is blank... his eyes dark. Anyone else would have been unnerved by his expression. But I know him. We are that familiar. I smile as I run my fingers lightly down the length of his chest to his tapered waist.

"What's wrong love? You need your muse?" I ask seductively... more than aware of what his answer will be. He

closes his eyes, obviously enjoying my touch. When he dares
open them again, they are even darker than before.

"Yes." The whisper of his husky voice conveys his
wants. He shifts his weight, spreading his legs further apart. He
reaches for my hair and pulls me in closer. Planted firmly
between his legs I can feel his growing desire. My breath catches
in my throat. It brings me pleasure, knowing that I can elicit that
kind of reaction from him. I lift my eyes to his beautiful,
chocolate face. Longingly, we stare at each other before either
of us move again. Could I ever tire of looking at him? The love
I have for him courses so deeply through my veins that my
heart aches just being near him. The fullness of his succulent
lips draws me in, enticing me to kiss them. I do just that, pulling
in his bottom lip into my waiting mouth. He moans in response,
tightening his grip on my hair. After I finish feasting on his
bottom lip, I work on his top one. He doesn't kiss me back,
allowing me to ravish him uninterrupted. His hand moves to the
nape of my neck, tracing it slightly with his fingertips. My body
instinctively tenses in response to his seductive touch. My
moans now match his own as we continue to explore through
the beautiful sensation of touch.

Light touches move from the nape of my neck to the
small of my back. My back arches as I gasp out loud. The want
has now transformed into a deep ache. Needing him to fill me
up completely, I reach for his jeans. My trembling hands make it
almost impossible to free him from the confining garment. As
the jeans reached his ankles, he expertly steps out of them,
never missing a beat on the task at hand. Finally, he kisses me
back, our tongues colliding in their orchestrated dance. Hands
now roam aimlessly, seeking pleasurable destinations. I grip his
swollen manhood and gently massage it. He, in turn caresses my
hardened nipples.

I can't take it anymore.

"Keenan please"I cry out. Without hesitation, he answers. Abruptly, he ends his assault on my nipples and grips my ass firmly in the palms of both hands. I expect him to pull me to the floor but instead he lifts me up and carries me to the nearest wall. Without bothering to remove my saturated panties, he simply moves them to the side and inserts his finger...his wondrous, slow massage causing me to cry out in ecstasy. I squirm beneath his touch, the pleasure so intense that it's almost unbearable. There is no escape as he pins me firmly with his free hand. I am completely at his mercy and I don't mind at all. He is so confident in loving me. I love that about him....the fact that he knows all of the things that drive me to the brink of insanity. I desperately try to hold on but he doesn't make it easy. He plants soft kisses my neck...my jawline before resting his face against my own.

"Let go baby." The breath of his alluring whispers leaves me whimpering. I can't hold on. I cry out his name as the first tremors begin.

"That's it sweetheart. Give it all to me." He continues to kiss my face. The tidal wave implodes as I give in, no longer in control over my own body.

*****

Exhausted...spent...I want nothing more than to collapse onto the floor. He does not allow me this luxury.

He releases my hands and removes his drenched fingers from my folds. His sculpted arms wrap easily around my waist. This newfound freedom allows me to grab fistfuls of his hair. I pulled him to me. I ravish his lips, suck his neck...feast on the heady mix of salt and sweat on his smooth chocolate skin. The raw hunger I have for this man is unlike any I have ever known with another. Somehow I always find myself wanting...more.

"I love you." My voice now hoarse with passion. "I love you baby...I love you." He groans in response to my declarations. I can feel his heat and hardness imposing against my slick skin. My pulse quickens as I moan in anticipation. He grabs my face and kisses me deeply before wrapping my legs around his narrow waist...entering me completely. My scream is deafening. Crazy...I don't think I could ever get used to the feel of him inside of my body. Each time just as amazing as the last. It never ceases to be...perfection.

Once again, he grabs my ass as he nibbles on my neck and shoulder. I arch my back... pushing me closer...pushing him deeper. He watches me with smoldering intensity.

"I love you." Unbridled truth rings in his words, leaving me breathless with emotion.

He moves...I move with him. He strokes...I push back. He bites...I claw. We both cry out each other's names. By the time he erupts, my body has already been wracked my multiple orgasms.

This time we both do collapse, exhausted and satisfied.

*****

Lauryn's haunting tone echoes through the house, as "Sweetest Thing" plays on repeat. The irony doesn't escape me. Keenan Jackson, my sweetest and best thing, is also my most complicated...thing.

I watch him as he sleeps. How could a love so magnificent in its existence be so...wrong? I roll over and head to the shower...suddenly feeling the need to wash away the remains of our last encounter.. The force of the pulsating water feels good pounding my aching body.

Still, my thoughts drift to our current situation. I don't want to alleviate my sexual high but I can't help but to worry about our future. I love him...in no uncertain terms. Any doubts about him not loving me no longer lingered. He is here and has proven himself with each passing day.

Is that enough though? There is still the matter of Sarai...his marriage. Until his divorce is settled, we will be forced to languish in limbo. A place I could never be comfortable residing. I just want to move forward with our lives but there are just so many steps to take before that process can even begin.

Step one: Getting past his parents. From my understanding, they will be in Atlanta in the next few weeks with his daughter. While he is excited about the visit with his daughter, I can tell that a level of apprehension exists beyond my level of comprehension. I think it's why he's been dealing with the mental block. He's stressing more than he wants to admit, but we are familiar enough for me to know his moods without an actual conversation.

I'm nervous as hell. How do you meet your boyfriend's parents when they're still calling someone else their daughter in law? How do they meet their son's future when his past has not been officially resolved? All grand questions that I have no answers to.

Especially painful is me knowing the impact our relationship will have on his daughter. For now we have both decided that I would not meet her. The timing just isn't right with so many other issues to deal with. It will be difficult enough just for her to deal with the news that her parents would no longer be together.

I hate this part of the story. I've been that kid and I still bear the emotional scars of being abandoned by my mother for her new lover. I never really forgave her and it's a hurdle that keeps us from being close even now. Now here I am, creating those same circumstances in another person's home. No, definitely not one of my proudest moments in life.

I sense his presence before he draws back the curtain.

"May I?" he asks, although he enters before I answer. His intrusion, though unsolicited, is a welcome diversion. My mind has been blanketed by enough confusion for the minute.

It's apparent that he senses my mood. "You good?"

"Yes," I answer quickly, not wanting the moment to be marred by tension. By the look on his face, I can tell that he's not convinced; nevertheless, he doesn't push the matter. Without saying anything, he turns me around and in expert fashion, runs his fingers through my hair. He massages my scalp, neck and shoulders. Unpleasant thoughts soon evaporate as I lose myself in the feel of his touch.

In this crazy love, I resign myself...perfect in all of its imperfections.

Chapter 27: Once My Brother

This has to be done. There's no way around it. If we are to exist, much less reside, in the same city, then it just has to be done. I refuse to hide. I've done far too much of that this past year and I won't to do it anymore. Somehow we have to figure this out...have the conversation...man to man...brother to brother.. It won't be easy. I know better than to hold my expectations that high. I know that it will take time to heal the wounds that I have inflicted...*we* have inflicted on each other. And honestly I don't know if they will ever completely heal. Sometimes you just go too far....do too much harm...to be able to get back. I do know that we have to try. If nothing else, we owe it to our familial bond to at least do that.

An intense and difficult conversation with my mom has left me laden with guilt. This fine mess is my doing. *All of it.* Everything that has transpired has been due to a domino effect that I, alone, have caused. I chose to leave D.C. I gave myself permission to get involved with Toni. I allowed her to fall in love with me...and I...I ultimately fell in love with her.

Do I regret it? I don't. If I could change anything, it would be the hurt, the pain, the brokenness...that my selfishness caused. Yet, if any of these scenarios result in me not getting to love her, then I don't...can't... regret it. All of this...is what I'll say to him...once my brother... my best friend. He deserves the truth and I won't insult him with sugar-coated lies.

We've agreed to meet at DJ's at Camp Creek. A bar wouldn't have been my first choice for a meeting of this magnitude. Dealing with people and loud voices competing with even louder TV's would not make for an ideal situation.

However, he has a business meeting out that way and the more I think about it, it makes sense to meet on neutral grounds.

When I enter the premise, I breathe a sigh of relief. The lunch crowd has dispersed; leaving only the stragglers occupying a few select booths and bar seats. The flat screens surrounding the bar and dining areas are on for casual viewing, but thankfully the volume is muted. A heavy-set bartender glances up when I enter and promptly instructs me to seat myself. He lumbers over to a side door that appears to lead to a back kitchen and calls out for "Toya" before resuming his stance at the bar. I do a quick scan of the room and notice an empty booth near the back. I figure it's in the perfect spot for me and Kyle to have our much-needed conversation. I'm not seated long before a waitress, identifying herself as "Toya", comes over to take my order. Before ordering food, I order a crown and coke, trying to ease my unsettled nerves.

Fifteen minutes later Kyle marches through the door. There is no handshake or brotherly hug. Instead, he slides in the booth and cautiously waits for me to speak. I could have never fathomed a day in which we would drift so far apart. Yet, here we are, barely speaking, our relationship holding on by the barest of threads.

Toya arrived with my drink and was about to get Kyle's order, but he declined. I took a long swig and let the thick dark liquid settle in my belly before speaking.

"Thank you for coming Kyle. I know you're busy."

Warily he searchs my face before responding. "What is this about Keenan? My meeting is in an hour."

The hostile tone of his voice takes me aback. It shouldn't but it does. I knew the moment he found out about me and Toni, our relationship would be altered...that the effects of the damage could be irreversible. I knew that when I decided to go to her. And I knew that the price may be too high to pay. My response is guarded.

"This...is about *her*, Kyle. It's always been about *her*."

He leans back, defensively folding his arms across his chest. "Why? Why are we going through the motions Keenan? You won. You got everything you wanted. No let me rephrase that...you *took* what you wanted. So no, we're not going to sit here and have a meaningless conversation about her? *She* is no longer a concern of mine."

Mindlessly, I shake the ice against my now empty glass. "I'm hoping to salvage something here Kyle. I know Toni hurt you...I know I did. Still, we're brothers man. I'm trying to gauge whether or not there's any part of us that can be saved. We owe each other that."

"Really?" he laughs. "I'm curious Keenan...exactly where was this concern for me...for our relationship...for your *wife*...when you fucked *her*?" His voice level raises a notch, garnering surreptitious glances from the scattered patrons.

"Don't say that...I *loved* her Kyle. I *tried*. I swear to God I tried man. What am I supposed to do? She's the love of my life. My *life*."

We sit in momentary silence...trying our best to digest the heavy words lacing the air.

"All I can hope is that when the anger subsides, and rationality returns you'll be willing to accept me back in your life. At the end of the day, we need each other...beyond *this*, we are still those boys...brothers...sitting on the stoop in Cherry Heights man."

He leans forward, his voice choked with emotion. "You betrayed me...*brother*. And there's nothing...nothing you can do, or say, that will *ever* make me forgive you for that."

The finality of his words hits home as I watch him grab his jacket and purposely walk out of the bar. We will see each other again...that's inevitable. Whether or not time will ever find us as brothers once more remains to be seen.

I make eye contact with Toya and signal for a refill. I might as well drown myself in sorrow, as the state of my new reality settles in.

Once my brother...now my enemy.

Chapter 28: Sunday Morning

Sunday morning. Most people in the south are waking up, preparing breakfast, getting the kids ready for Sunday school and then church. Although I have been in Atlanta for months, I still have not fallen victim to these traditions. Instead, I am doing the only thing that eases my mind when it's in a troubled state.

Work.

The building is quiet except for Frank, the lone security officer standing guard in the main lobby. I take a few minutes to chat with him; with the hours I put in, we know each other well. I take the elevator to our floor and settle in for what I hope to be a long, productive day. I need this, the pages, the numbers, the calculations, the client reviews. This...my process that will propel me back to the business of living.

It hasn't been easy. When Keenan left D.C. to move to Atlanta with Kyle, I was broken. I was in complete disbelief that the fractures in our relationship were that irreparably damaged. All of my life, I had been that girl. The one who always had a plan and an outline of what life would be. When I met Keenan on Howard's campus, he seemed the perfect fit for my scheme. Obviously easy on the eyes, he was also ambitious and excited about his future. God, he even had a wonderful relationship with his mother.

After we married, the other critical pieces all fell into place. We got our dream jobs, moved into our first house, and had our beautiful, perfect daughter.. Life was good, really good.

Then it changed. He changed. Evidence of the first cracks appeared. I just needed him to be the man I married...but... he changed. His dreams, goals, and outlook on life...it all became different, while I was left with the daunting task of redefining the man I loved.

Regardless, I always had hope that we could make it right. Even when he wanted space, I gave in, naively confident that he would find his way back home.

This time it's different.

When he walked out of the door to our makeshift home, I was faced with the blinding reality that he was never coming back...that my carefully constructed family would forever remain...broken.

It didn't hit me then, when I sat drunken...transfixed at the dining room table. No, it didn't hit me until two days later, when I spoke to my baby girl on the phone and with child-like enthusiasm, she asked for 'daddy'. I lost it, and went in search of the only person who could even begin to understand my pain...*Kyle*. Mentally, he was in worse shape than I was, however, by the time I left we were both...better. At least I was. There is comfort in knowing that I'm not in the fight alone.

Keenan and I have not spoken, although we will need to have a conversation really soon. There are intricate steps to this process of separation. Steps, which I'm not quite ready to take. I'll get there, albeit, in my own time. Keenan will want to get this resolved as soon as possible so that he can move on with *her*, but I've already decided that I won't give him that satisfaction, or her for that matter. That may seem petty...vengeful even, but it is my last card to play.

Her.

I hate her....everything about her. The very fact that she is the complete opposite of who I am makes this situation even more difficult to bear. It seems impossible that the same man could fall in love with the both of us. That alone, is a testament as to how much he's changed. Or maybe he is who he has been all along. It's painful to think of the possibility that she gets to live life with the real Keenan; even more painful to think that he, the man I so deeply loved, is one who 'settled' for me.

The sound of footsteps interrupts my train of thought. I look up just in time to see Marcus coming down the long hallway, dressed unusually casual in jeans, sneakers and tee. Even dressed down, he is remarkably handsome. I'm not surprised to see him. Kindred spirits he and I. Back in D.C. the two of us frequently shared early mornings and late nights in the office. Me, always trying to get one step ahead...him, always trying to maintain his position. It's how we have built our bond, although, for obvious reasons, we try to keep our exact closeness under wraps.

He walks directly into my office and hands me, what I can only assume, is a double shot latte and a small brown paper bag. Inside is a blueberry muffin from one of my favorite cafes on the corner. I smile at him graciously as he settles into one chair and carelessly props his feet on the other.

"Morning and thank-you."

His magnificent smile is a ray of light on this otherwise gloomy morning.

"Morning."

So is the beginning of an ordinary conversation. For at least an hour we talk about everything other than work. I am glad to have this moment to escape my own thoughts. My moment of reprieve; however, does not last long.

"So, lady, are you going to tell me why you're here instead of at home with Keenan?"

Initially, I don't give in to his inquisition. It is not my intention to get that deep today.

Not to be deterred, Marcus continues. "I know I'm pushing boundaries, being all in your business, but I know the toll your work ethic puts on your marriage. While I appreciate you for giving the agency your best efforts, I just want you to keep in mind that you will need to find work-life balance. I don't want to see you repeating some of those same mistakes."

I can't believe the words coming out of his mouth. Surely Marcus Paul, the man, the myth, the legend...who's known for his extreme work ethic, is not really telling me to find work-life balance.

"Before you decide to get too critical about my personal life," I retaliate, "I just want to remind you Mr. Paul, that you are the only other person, besides Frank, in this building with me on a Sunday morning."

His abrupt laughter is full and rich. "Ok you got me. However, there is a difference. I don't have a wife or kids, for that very reason. You, my friend, have both."

Again I don't respond. I don't know how. At some point people will know that my marriage has disintegrated, but I'm not sure if I'm ready to put it in the atmosphere just yet. There is humiliation in failure. And in my case there's even more humiliation in knowing that my husband purposely chose to love someone else.

I decide to take a chance on telling Marcus. Better now that later when the real chaos begins.

"Had."

There is confusion in his eyes.

"I don't understand."

"Had...Keenan and I aren't together anymore." There, the words are spoken out loud. Maybe now my brain can truly begin to process it and my heart, maybe my heart will begin to follow.

He sits up straight in the chair. I continue to sip my coffee...and patiently wait. Truthfully, I don't know how he'll react. He is my friend. The Paul Agency is his business, his life. I know him; he will worry if I can handle the stress of the separation compounded with the brutal task of building the new office.

Finally he responds. "Sarai, I am so sorry to hear that. Damn, I've watched you over the years try to keep it all together. I pushed you hard, made a lot of demands...I hope to God none of that had an impact."

"Of course not Marcus. Me and Keenan...we just somehow got off course and could never get back on track. You want to hear something ironic. He left me for Rayna's best friend, the woman I told you about before. So technically, I am the reason for the demise of my own marriage."

"Because you brought him back." The realization hits him. My silence is his confirmation. For a while there are no words, the weight of circumstances a heavy burden.

"Sarai, this isn't on you. Forgive me for saying this, but Keenan has never appreciated you like he should. In my opinion he bailed out early in the game. The fact that we've only been here a few months before he's gone...again...speaks volumes about his character. He doesn't deserve you." There is an unmistakable trace of anger in his voice.

While still stewing in my own anger, somehow I find myself getting defensive about the man, who for now, I still legally claim as husband.

"He's not all bad Marcus. I mean, he's a great father, and there was a time that he was a wonderful husband as well. I don't know...it seems crazy but my emotions are in such conflict."

There is a curious expression on his face as he stares at me. At least it isn't a piteous one. I can't take any sense of pity.

"Well, if anything that only serves to prove my point. He doesn't deserve you Sarai. He's much too...weak...of a man for a woman like you."

I don't answer. In many ways everything he's saying is true. Keenan absolutely proved to be a weak man...much weaker than I ever anticipated.

"Anyway..." he starts, in an obvious attempt at redirecting the conversation. "How will this impact your work here?"

Marcus Paul. At the end of the day, it always comes back to business...always. Knowing his true nature, understanding it...I can't find offense in his frankness. It's one characteristic that I've always admired and respected. At least with him, I never have to wonder about where I stand.

"No worries my friend. I'm here. None of this mess will impact my work. I'm beyond all that."

"I hope so Sarai. To be frank, I worry about how all of this will affect your working relationship with Rae. When I return to D.C., I have to know that I'm leaving this branch running as a well-oiled machine. The two of you together have great potential."

Again I don't answer. I don't want to think about Rayna. Any thoughts I entertain of her will naturally progress to thoughts of Toni. Thoughts of Toni will bring the anger, that I've been trying to keep submerged, bubbling to the surface. At this point, I can't allow that kind of exposure. To unleash it in its entirety would mean relinquishing any control that I've struggled to maintain.

In due time Sarai.

"Sarai." His seat stands deserted as reaches out for me. With slight reluctance, I reach back. He pulls me out of my chair and unexpectedly encases me in a strong, masculine embrace. This strange display of affection catches me off guard. His heat, his smell...it's unfamiliar. Yet, being in his arms brings me some level of comfort.

The success you've been fighting for is right here...right within reach. Don't let Keenan steal this from you. He's taken enough already."

His words ring somewhat true. Keenan's weakness ultimately led to the demise of our family. I won't make allowances for that. He failed, and that betrayal will eventually come with its own price, that he alone will have to pay. However, as far as I'm concerned, Toni is the real thief. She took what wasn't rightfully hers to take...my husband, my life.

My mother's voice rises from the darkness of my mind, "You've been a damn fool Sarai."

Yes, yes I have. Foolishness and naiveté have often plagued my past, but they will have no place in my future. I refuse to be anyone's fool or victim, least of all Toni. When the smoke clears and all is said and done, she will realize that she won this battle, but the war...the war has just begun.

Chapter 29: The Endgame

"Why such a solemn face? You should be over the moon. This is *the* day."

The rich voice belongs to Daniel. We are gathered in his office to finalize the paperwork for Muse. Even through the cloud of my somber mood, I can detect his excitement. He has every right to be. The grand opening for the new location will officially happen in one month. Several months behind schedule, nevertheless, we're *there*...the light at the end of the tunnel.

I should be ecstatic. Rather, I'm just...exhausted.

This project has been more of an undertaking than I initially anticipated. In fact, it's not even the same project as when we began. What started as a plan for opening a second location somehow transformed into a proposal to close the original location of Muse, then rebuild and rebrand it all on a more grand scale.

In truth, I still harbor misgivings on how it all went down, which in some ways accounts for my present state of mind. It was a move orchestrated by our new partners Morial Investment Group (MIG), a fairly new start-up in the Metro Atlanta area. Deciding to go with a new company was risky. However, it had proven difficult to obtain the necessary funding to get our project off the ground. Morial was backed with verified money; however, their investment didn't come without a price. From our first meeting with their representative, it was clear they had no interest in being silent partners. They came to the table with a voice. They came with demands.

Their first order of business was to nix the idea of maintaining two locations. From their perspective, it didn't make sound financial sense. After many heated discussions, numerous threats to walk away, and strategic mediation from Daniel, Tanya and I eventually gave in and moved forward.

As the old wooden and glass doors to Muse were locked and latched for the last time, my heart broke. Mentally, I had accepted that greater was coming; however, emotionally I was unprepared. Beyond those brick walls was a space that held a lifetime of memories a new building couldn't capture. Me and Tanya's excitement at our first grand opening, my morning coffee in my worn booth, Mia's first night blessing the stage, spontaneous lunches with Rae and Dawn, the day Keenan walked into the space and forever changed my life...intimate and confidential conversations with Kyle.

Kyle.

It still hurts to think of him. I suppose it always will. As I stood in the center of the floor on that last night, echoes of our long-ago conversations haunted me. I'm sure the whispers will linger long after the doors are locked and the blinds drawn.

I miss my friend...my best friend. We have not spoken since the day he walked out of my house a broken man. Rae, Mia, and Dawn try to keep me abreast of his well-being, but sometimes those conversations are just too hard, and much too awkward.

Many times throughout this frustrating process, I've mindlessly picked up the phone to call him. He's always been there...my constant, my shoulder, my comforter. Then reality sets in and I remember. "We" don't exist anymore. Life, as it once was, no longer exists.

Keenan is my future and I don't regret for one minute following through with that decision. Nevertheless, for almost half of my life, another man shared my past. He was...everything and it's been a major adjustment dealing with life without him. With time it will get easier, though I can't kid myself. It will never be the same.

"Are you with me Ms. Charles?" Daniel's voice chimes in again. I finally turn to face him.

"Forgive me Daniel. My mind is all over the place today."

"I can tell. You barely heard a word I said. What's going on?"

"Nothing really," I start, unsure of how to continue. The proceedings are about to begin and I don't want to weigh him down with my emotions. Besides, we make great business partners, but our relationship has never really developed beyond that.

"This is all so...much. Hopefully, my anxiety level will settle down after the papers are signed and the grand opening is over and done with. I'm just ready to get past this state of limbo."

Before he can respond, Alexander "Alex" Brecken, general counsel for MIG, enters the room, soon followed by Tanya, who had stepped out earlier to make a call. Tanya instantly heads in our direction. Alex, meanwhile, sets up his briefcase and papers at the head of the long oak table before walking over to greet us. He moves with an air of confidence that contradicts his reserved image: glasses, small stature, and pale, almost translucent skin.

He shakes hands with Daniel before leaning in to kiss my cheek. Funny how we've come full circle. At the beginning of this process I treated him like public enemy number one. Since then, I've actually grown to respect him. While I haven't agreed with most of the decisions of his firm, I've come to at least appreciate the knowledge and expertise he brings to the table.

243

"I'm fine," Daniel answers. "Toni's nerves are a little on edge though."

Tanya replies, "I have to admit, I've been a nervous wreck all morning. It's...real now."

Alex gives us both a reassuring smile. "That's to be understood. Make no mistake...this is a big deal. One swipe of the almighty pen and your lives will be forever changed. With MIG's financial backing, Muse is primed to become one of the more premier venues in Atlanta. Give it about two years and you both will see more money than you've seen before in this business. Every time you start to feel anxious, just think about that."

"I know." Tanya responds. "There's just so much riding on this going right. Y'all know I'm a single mom. My endgame is to ensure that my son's future is stable...secure."

"Well as soon as all of the partners get here, we'll get right to business. There's no reason to prolong the matter any further. You ladies did review the packets I sent over right? We'll tackle any last minute questions or concerns, but at this point it should just be a matter of getting everyone's Hancocks on the dotted lines."

"Yes." Daniel answers. We've spent the past week reviewing everything with attorneys. I think we're prepared." As he speaks, he looks to me and Tanya for reassurance. We both smile and nod.

It's time to move forward.

The door opens once again, and Faith, Daniel's Executive Assistant, escorts a male and female into the room. I recognize their faces from one prior meeting, although their exact names escape me at the moment.

With our primary point of contact being Alex, there are still partners we have not been privileged to meet. As they begin to file in and occupy the space, I wonder if today will be that day.

Tanya, Daniel, and I move to the chairs closer to the windows. Alex moves to his self-designated seat and starts passing down folders which include the final copies of the contract he had sent over to us to preview. Filled with nervous energy, I start reading the packet again, ensuring that no additional language had been added.

While my mind is focused on the words of the pages, I hear a voice that sounds vaguely familiar. I glance up and I'm shocked to see Marcus Paul. He greets Alex and the other partners with a smile and handshakes before turning his attention to our group.

Or it seems, specifically towards me.

"Toni." The coolness of his tone indicates the strictest professionalism. There is no hint of the warmth he displayed at Copeland's. No sign of the man who laughed, joked, and shared casual conversations and drinks at our table.

My heart drops to my stomach. *Why is he here?*

I turn helplessly to Tanya and Daniel, who both appear just as confused.

"Marcus." The words somehow escape my throat. "What are you doing here?"

Alex overhears the conversation and promptly steps in. "Well I see you all have officially met. Marcus, meet the people behind the files: Tanya, Toni, and Daniel. I'd hoped to get you all together before now but the schedule has been crazy hectic. Marcus Paul everyone, the owner and founder of The Paul Agency and the man instrumental in pulling this group of investors together. You'll be spending a lot of time together. Marcus plans to be very hands on this first year."

Marcus Paul...a primary partner in MIG? How can this be happening? Before I can fully recover and wrap my head around the events taking place, Faith escorts another man into the room. I stand, completely startled, sending my chair colliding into the back wall.

"Kyle." My voice is a straggled whisper. I haven't seen him in months. He's leaner than when I last saw him, still handsome, but...harder, somehow. There's such a harsh coldness in his eyes and deliberate purpose in his steps as he strides over to join the party assembled at the table.

"Daniel, Tanya." In an ultimate display of disrespect, he does not speak my name. Tears spring to my eyes. Even after all of this time, he still hates me so much. My best friend hates me.

Daniel and Tanya both stand in a defiant show of support. Alex, as well as the other partners present, have now gauged that *something* is happening.

"What the hell is going on?" Daniel seethes, staring directly at Kyle. In rare form, his entire body is taut with tension and anger.

Alex, typically so confident, shies away in confusion, suddenly realizing there are elements at play that do not involve him.

Instead of Kyle answering, Marcus takes the reins. "Well you all know Kyle Jordan right? He's another investor in the group. Through the professional 'network', he heard that you all were having problems coming up with the funding for your project. We figured we'd pool our resources, build our group, and...bail you out. Seems like a worthwhile investment."

The walls of the room are slowly closing in. I try to take deep breaths to keep a rising panic attack at bay. No, he wouldn't do this, he wouldn't be this cruel.

"Kyle, don't do this...I know you hate me...and I deserve that. But you can't own a piece of Muse. It's *mine*. My sweat, my dedication, my... life. You...can't...do...this."

I look for something, anything in his demeanor to indicate that some sense of rationality is present. There's nothing...nothing. Flat, emotionless eyes stare back at me.

"Kyle! Answer me. Look at me. You *loved* me."

"Ah...love...a funny, funny thing that love is. In the grand scheme of things...it's really nothing at all."

I recognize the silky voice even before I see her face or that rebellious red hair. Defeated...broken, I cover my face with my hands.

Sarai.

She warned me to keep that door closed. She warned me that if I came for him, she would make me regret it. I didn't listen. For that, she's made me pay the ultimate price.

She's stolen Muse...taken my life.

The chickens have indeed come home to roost.

Note to Reader:

Thank you for continuing this journey with me! It's been a long time coming but I hope the wait was worth it. As an artist, it brings me immense joy to bring this story and these characters into your lives. I hope you have come to love (or hate) them as much as I do. Your patience, loyalty, and unwavering support are greatly appreciated. Without YOU there is no ME. Much love.

LAKINIA RAMSEY is a native of Desoto (Sumter County), GA, who currently resides in Austin, TX. She attended Georgia Southwestern State University in Americus, GA where she obtained an MBA (Management) and a BA in Political Science. Throughout her professional career, she has worked with diverse families and the homeless population served in the roles of manager, advocate and case manager in the social service, criminal justice, and non-profit arenas. She is the Co-Founder of Abstract Village, an organization that supports artists and projects through the "Be the Village" Fund. Previous works include her first novel, Good Intentions, and other works as a free-lance writer and web content creator and editor. Upcoming projects include Good Intentions 3: Motivation, the screenplay for Good Intentions, and a stage-play tentatively titled "Middle Row Blues."

Good Intentions 2:
Blind Ambition
(Reader's Guide)

1. What's your opinion on this sequel? Do you feel it stayed true to the original story arc?

2. Do you recognize any continuing themes from Book 1? Can you identify them?

3. Do you feel that the characters have evolved in any way since Book 1? If so, in what ways?

4. In what ways can you identify theme: "Blind Ambition" throughout the book?

5. In this book, Sarai's character has a more prominent role. What do you feel about her character and the choices she make? Do you think you would have made any of the same decisions?

6. How do you feel about the character and role of Marcus Paul? What are your thoughts on the relationship between him and Sarai?

7. What do you feel about Toni and Kyle's relationship? How has it evolved? Do you think there's any chance of their relationship being redeemed in the future?

8. Do you think Keenan should have stayed with his family out of a sense of obligation or do you feel that he made the right decision to follow his heart?

9. Did the book end the way you expected?

10. Would you recommend this book to others?

Good Intentions 3:

Motivation

--*Reflections, Mia Scott*

What is love? How do you define it? All of my life I've been told that true love is unconditional...that it loves beyond faults, sometimes beyond reason. It may wane in its intensity, but never dissipates. Always...constant.

I don't know that kind of love. It's never existed in my world. Doesn't mean that I haven't yearned for it. I've wanted to experience it. To be draped in its silkiness. To carry a little piece of it with me every day like a good luck charm. To know that regardless of what I'm going through in life, it is there...waiting in the wings...to carry me, to uplift me, to support me...or to rejoice with me. I wanted it...but it has remained at bay.

So I stopped searching for it a long time ago.

I've been deceived by illusions. Many times, I've thought I had discovered it. In the early morning lying in the arms of lovers, in poetic whisperings, in butterfly touches, in promises void of truth. Yet, in time, what I believed to be real was always revealed to be a lie.

Always.

So now I'm done. I'm done searching for this evasive "love." This thing that seems to always be just beyond the reach of my fingertips. I can live without it, exist without it. Without the lies...without the deceit.

I've seen the damages left in its wake and I won't be a willing victim. I was naïve once, but not anymore. I can't be. This world has proven to be cold. People break your heart, they betray you, and they take what they want.

Well Mia Scott can play this game with the best of them. That young, naïve girl is no more. I'm a grown ass woman, and I'm here to prove to the world that I am a force to be reckoned with.

They will see.

252

Made in the USA
Columbia, SC
17 May 2019